In a Parallel Universe

By
Samar Saadallah

Disclaimer
This is a work of fiction. Any names and\or resemblance to actual persons, living or dead, is entirely coincidental.

Dedication

I dedicate this book,
To any woman or girl,
Who has experienced any harm,
For simply existing as female.
I see you,
I hear you,
You are never alone.

Mariam
Part One

I gasp for air and try to relish the feeling of breathing again, but I find that I don't need to. I do not seem to need oxygen running through my lungs. "Where am I?" is the first coherent thought I can decipher. I glance around only to find that I am lying on my own bed. I recognize it instantly. The place where I had felt most at home, but just as estranged.

I should have panicked until I couldn't breathe. I remember that feeling clearly. But it doesn't happen. I signal for my hands to lift so I can look at them, but they do not seem to be there. I get up and walk to the old standing mirror - I remember how happy I felt the day my parents got it for me. I look in the mirror, but do not see my reflection. My long dark brown hair and bangs. My equally dark eyes. The mole I despise. All the things that used to define me. The mirror stares back at me, mockingly empty. I realize I do not have a physical existence anymore. My body is gone.

I stand there for what seems like an eternity, unable to do anything else, studying the reflection of my room, which seems to lack nothing but my presence. After a while, I regain the ability to perceive and move again, and notice for the first time that my room *does* look different. Some items are covered with a dusty white yellowing sheet and an air of neglect. Since the furniture is now masked in white, and this is the color of the walls, it seems beautiful to me, peaceful even, yet haunting. All my belongings are gone. The perfumes on my dresser, the notebooks on my always-cluttered desk, the picture frame that used to be on my nightstand displaying a picture of me and my parents when I was a kid, huddled together on my grandmother's sofa. My mom's timid smile. My father's unsmiling face.

For the second time, I feel like I should have experienced the panic sensation at this moment, but again I don't. *Where are my parents?* I rush to the window and notice that the thick green curtains have been removed. Perhaps I am in this alternative reality, which resembles my room? Maybe this is not my house at all. Maybe this is all a strangely realistic dream. The thought fills me with a mixture of hope and dread. I glance out of the window, and the reality of it sinks into whatever my existence is.

This isn't a dream. It isn't an alternative universe. This really is my home. The narrow, crowded street hasn't changed at all. The soft bluish hue of the early morning covers the place in an aura of peace, which seems to clash severely with the ceaseless action happening on its uneven and aging asphalt. A young man with pant legs rolled up is splashing water out of a dirty red bucket and into the air right in front of the fruit stand. Women and men are emerging from building entrances and rushing to begin their days. The world outside is grinding to a start. The world is moving and I'm not.

Loathing is what I think I should be feeling right now. At least, that is what I remember feeling when looking out of this window before I ended up the way I am right now.

I turn away and have another would-be panic attack before moving on. Room after room I enter, checking to see if anything has changed. This does not take much time, as I have no physical body slowing me down.

Everything is in the same place. The furniture is there, but covered in dusty sheets, just like it is in my room. My parents haven't sold the place, but they don't seem to have lived here for quite a while. Where could they have gone? And what had become of them after I was gone? I have no idea, and I am afraid to find out.

What now? For the first time ever, I do not know what is required of me to do or the rules and expectations I must follow. I look around at the only room I have not yet explored. I examine the spacious salon, as if waiting for it to tell me what to do, but it stares back speechless, unfazed. If I could smell right now, I wonder if the familiar scent of my father's musk cologne mixed with the smell of old carpets would linger around me. Instead, I can feel a peculiar vibe emanating from my old home. Abandonment. A fading, almost non-existent comfort.

I wonder why they did not take any of the furniture with them. The large pastel blue sofa is still sitting there where it has been all my life. For seventeen years, it was always in the middle of the room, with its back against the largest window. I can almost see me as a five-year-old, jumping up and down on it, bursting with childish glee until a high-pitched cry of joy escaped me, my mom coming over, her eyebrows holding onto each other as if in a firm handshake, raised in anger. But she can't keep a straight face, so I jump off the sofa into her arms, and she hugs me so tightly, so safely. I can almost hear our mingled laughter. Almost see her round face and midnight-black hair, eyes crinkled at the corners when she smiles.

But there is no laughter and she isn't here, and the girl I used to be doesn't exist anymore. I cannot bear to stay where I am any longer. And I do not want to remember any of it. The longer I stay, the more it starts to come back to me. I want to think of nothing. I want to *be* nothing. What a powerful word 'nothing' is. A scary and enticing prospect I have longed for, for a long, long time. I just want to be a floating cloud, free of emotion, so light, so effortless. I do not want to exist, at least not as me. So I decide that this nothingness is what I am going to be.

Farha

In a parallel universe, the rest of her life would be hers to orchestrate into a melody of her own.

Her mother called her name over and over again for what seemed like an eternity. "Farha, Farha, Farha!" Her name ceased to make sense; instead, it seemed like a random combination of sounds that didn't concern her. Farha had locked herself into the only room in the house. Her mother banged on the door, the only barrier keeping Farha's sanity intact. It brought her thoughts back from kilometers away, but she ignored the increasing thumps, as if they were somewhere unreachable. Glistening tears filled her Mediterranean-blue eyes, the same ones that caused all those who crossed her path to say, "*Masha' Allah!* They are as precious as diamonds," when in reality, they were merely magnets for unwarranted stares.

She scanned the room, her thoughts racing faster than her eyes, which came to a halt, dazzled by the droplets of sun that danced on the dark floor. She noticed how the spots were created by the growing spaces between the decaying shutters, which her memory told her had once been a pistachio green, but now were as vaguely dust-colored as the rest of the house. The lights flickered and danced, unaware and unbothered by her problems. But she knew that was the thing about nature. Even when she thought one moment to be the end of the world, nature carried on unceasingly with or without you. As if on command, the wind struggled to blow, burdened by the weight of the humidity that exerted its presence, like a living thing. It reached Farha's face, touched it enticingly, pulling her thoughts to the day that started it all.

————·◆◆ ◆ ◆◆·————

That day had also been just as humid. The start of it had been normal, free of any signs of what was to come. At Al Zahraa School for Girls, the only one within miles, the Arabic teacher, Mrs. Hanaa, droned on and on, repeating a poem from the curriculum that was so boring that the words melted together in Farha's head, creating a big blob of sound. So Farha surreptitiously read her own books instead, placing them between the pages of her schoolbook. She would read the school poem later, just before the exam as usual. Listening to Mrs. Hanaa repeat it time and again, getting louder each time, didn't help. Studying was almost effortless for Farha. Most of the subjects relied on memorization anyway. Her schoolbooks never excited her; only her own books did.

Years ago, her third primary teacher, and probably her favorite person, Mrs. Soha, noticed that Farha's IQ was much higher than her colleagues'. That was when she started to lend Farha books from her own collection, and Farha devoured them like sunflower seeds. Mrs. Soha had long since moved to Cairo, but Farha kept on reading. She read everything she could get her hands on, from history and art to philosophy and astronomy. But her favorite genre was always fiction. Any fiction. If it was an interesting book, Farha couldn't wait to read it. If there were interesting worlds, she wanted to go there. If there were interesting characters, she wanted to meet them or be them. If there was an interesting plot, she wanted to melt into it. Books were her only escape from a life that was as dull and stagnant as a mosquito-infested lake. Because where there were books, there were possibilities, and that was always what kept Farha going: the existence of possibilities.

The only problem was getting her hands on these books. The village did not have a single bookstore, but Farha wouldn't give up on her books so easily. That was when she befriended *Am* Abdo, the old grocery-store owner, and figured out that on his trips to other governorates, he could get her the books she wanted. To request one or two books at the end of the month, Farha would save almost every penny her parents gave her. Then to avoid raising suspicions, she would only read outside the house and claim to be out with a friend. But, in reality, Farha's only friends were fictional. But that didn't upset her at all. In fact, that day, she couldn't wait to get to her secret reading spot in the village to meet them.

On her walk back from school, reaching her reading spot was her main motivation, and she wanted to get there as quickly as possible. As usual, she passed the biggest cornfield in the village on her right, and the busy market, a blur of movement, on her left. Not paying much attention to her surroundings, Farha walked on with a barely detectable childish skip in her step. And that was when, seemingly out of nowhere, she ran into something.

Taken aback by the sudden impact, she quickly bent down to pick up her books. While she struggled to collect up her belongings, she looked up at the cause, and was surprised to see that it was a man. He had deep wrinkles, engraved into his forehead like canals making their way across the empty field of his expressionless face. He seemed to be in his fifties, probably older than her father. His broad shoulders and height added to his intimidating demeanor. They made him look even more threatening against her petite, not-quite-woman-yet frame. But most noticeable about him were his eyes. They lacked any emotion and moved eerily, like a Nile crocodile scanning the perimeter.

He looked down at the scared fourteen-year-old girl in his wake. Farha gathered the rest of her books, scrambled to her feet, and walked away swiftly, afraid even to utter an apology. As she walked away, she turned around slightly only to see him inquire about her from the pencil-thin man from the nearby *qahwa*.

It seemed like an uncomfortable yet forgettable interaction at the time, but little did she know what was to come.

That night, Farha teased her younger brother, Ahmed, in the bedroom. Theirs was a relationship that was a hybrid between a mother and her son and two siblings that lived to annoy each other. After all, she and bursting-with-energy Ahmed were the only two unmarried siblings left. She could faintly hear her father debate something with a deep-voiced stranger outside, but dismissed the matter as unimportant. A while later, her mother walked into the room.

"Ahmed, go to your father. He needs your help with something."

"What does he want?" Ahmed grumbled.

"Go. Now!"

Ahmed mumbled some words under his breath and left.

Farha felt an imminent unease. Her mother started to speak casually, but to Farha, it was as if every sentence removed part of the ground from under her feet.

"Your father and I were just talking to a man. A merchant from a nearby town who is now in the village doing business. A respectable man. He says he saw you at the market today and immediately knew he wanted to ask for your hand in marriage."

She paused, as if waiting for any cue as to how to continue, but Farha sat there unmoving, eyes glued to her mother, refusing to hint at emotion.

So her mother went on. "Your father gave him his word of approval. Personally, I also think it's a good idea. He seems very well off and can provide for you. You will be better off than all your sisters. Oh, why are you giving me that face? You should be happy!"

Farha's eyes welled up with tears.

"This is not the time to cry. You are too old for this."

"But Mama -"

"Look, I know this is a bit sudden, but your father already gave his word, so there is nothing to talk about."

"But what about me? Shouldn't I have a say in this?!"

"Lower your voice, or do you want your father to hear you? We know what is best for you, and it does not get better than a man who has more than enough means to care for you and your children, put a roof over your head and more than enough food on the table. That is all you can wish for in this life. The neighbor's daughters and anyone in this village would kill for a groom like this. I'm not even going to talk about it to anyone until it's a done deed to avoid the evil eye. Don't be ungrateful."

"Mama, please … you … you don't understand." Farha was finding it hard to form sentences between heaving sobs. "I … I don't want to get married now. I like going to school. I like my life as it is now. I don't want to get married, please. Please don't do this."

"It is decided, Farha. You don't know what is best for you now, but someday you are going to thank us for this."

Farha couldn't speak anymore. Her mother leaned over and hugged her. She didn't hug her mother back.

Incoherent thoughts filled her mind, trying to cloak themselves with denial as if ashamed of their very existence.

His lifeless eyes.

His greedy hands, ever so eager to buy fresh merchandise.

Her mother.

Hands baking fresh *baladi* bread in the morning.

The smell of home.

Her mother caring for her bleeding wound when she had fallen down when she was seven.

Her mother braiding her hair every morning before school.

Her mother … selling her off to a complete stranger.

A stranger.

Nothing makes sense.

Farha noticed her hands were shaking, her breathing more rapid, her heart beating too fast. Her mother being around had always meant warmth; a perfectly prepared cup of tea, an embrace more sheltering than the brittle walls they called home. Even when she yelled, her mother, to Farha, had meant safety. Her brain tried and faltered in attempting to make the connection between the mother she thought she knew and the person who was in front of her.

And even her father. He was a man who was always physically there, but somehow always distant. A man who knew only how to put food on the table, but never showed her tenderness. She was the only one in the family who had his eyes, but a real connection between them had never existed. But no, even he wouldn't do this. She wondered if she finally understood why he never showed her any love. Maybe he had always seen her as a burden, and she wished she could go back to a time when that thought was not stitched into her brain as it was now.

Farha spent many hours crying into her pillow so that no one would hear her, until she eventually fell asleep.

As the date of the wedding approached, the fourteen-year-old refused to eat. She sat on her bed for days, rebelling against the union by refusing to eat or move. Her parents seemed to think she was mad, and had given up on trying to talk to her. Her four older sisters had accepted their fates in eerily similar fashions. They had left their home for the last time as young girls, fear hidden behind accepting eyes, and returned as mothers, and the light that used to exist in their eyes was dimmer. The four of them seemed to have love for their children, but none had come to have feelings for their husbands, or so Farha had observed.

The wedding day was here. The drops of sunlight continued to dance on the floor, but Farha was lying in bed, unmoving. Her mother continued to shout her name in an attempt to force her to get up and get ready for the ceremony. No other words had made the effect her mother wanted, so she resorted to just using her daughter's name. But Farha heard none of it. In her head a battle was raging: *is it even possible to escape?*

Out of nowhere, realizations washed over her like freezing water on a cold winter night. She didn't care whether she ended up being shot by the man or her own father for the sake of honor. She didn't care if trying to escape was almost suicidal. A future that seemed entirely free of possibility. A future she could picture now from beginning to end because of how many times she had seen it happen to other girls. That future, and that fate, to her, was worse than death.

Slowly, she tried to get up. Her entire body shook. She was weak from hunger. Dizzy stars and galaxies appeared before her eyes. Regardless, she managed to get up and then put one foot in front of the other, and walked out of the room to what seemed to be all the women of her family seated on the floor. All her aunts were there. Even her cousins, whom she only saw on special occasions, were there, and so were her sisters and their children. In return, she was met with curious eyes studying her carefully, trying to make sense of her appearance. She mustered all the strength she had left into a faint and painful smile. Her mother asked her if she was ready. Farha nodded.

With those words, her mother, sisters and neighbors exploded into excited ululations, blessings, and shared embraces. Farha knew the wedding was to be held soon anyway, whether or not the bride had given her consent, but they all seemed happy that they didn't have to force anything. It was less of a fuss that way.

The wedding was going to be held in the village, and she was to be prepared at her house. Then she would be taken away to her husband's hometown, where he already had two wives and their children.

First, she was presented with a large serving of *feteer* and the foul-smelling aged cheese she had always despised, but for the first time in her life, she inhaled it with all the hunger that had been gnawing at her flesh and sanity for days. Her mother watched with what Farha thought was a hint of sadness, and then, just as suddenly, it was gone.

"Your life will be comfortable and full of luxury, unlike our own," her mother said.

Farha remained silent, looking at the floor, and her stomach grumbled, as if the aged cheese had lodged itself there.

"You are making the reasonable choice. I'm confident everything will work out well," her mother assured her. "Your father and I, we got married in the same way. Look at us now. We have many children, we are surviving, and most of our children are married too. What more could there possibly be to life? You're just scared, but this will all fade away, and you will be thankful."

Farha thought of a hundred replies. She thought about telling her how satisfied and content she was with the life they had given her. She thought about screaming and asking her if she had ever complained about anything at all. She thought about crying and begging and pleading for her mother to reconsider. Instead, she added them all to the list of things she would never get to say, because she had tried time and again to beg them to not marry her off. It only ended with her mother disappointingly looking at the floor and her father threatening to lock her up or beat some sense into her. Her face had endured far too many slaps since the day when that man had walked into her family's house.

The ladies of the family then descended upon her from all directions, and suddenly her body was not her own. It was a product that had to meet the standards of its buyer. And so they brushed her hair and washed her body, and pulled at her body hair with sticky paste. Almost everything they did was painful, but she had been told many times that in the life of a woman, pain was a companion that would only leave her when her body met the grave.

And so far, it had been true. At the moment, she could stomach the pain of their preparations, but it unlocked a memory of a much worse one. Farha vaguely remembered her circumcision procedure. It was as though her brain had erased most of what had happened that day, knowing that she couldn't handle one second of a clear memory of it in her head. But even though her memory had faded, her body hadn't forgotten. She only remembered up until the moment her mother had taken her to a clinic in the village. Then, all she could recall were her own screams until she passed out. Everything else was the closest shade of gray to black. She had asked her mother years after the event why she had done it, and her mother had told her it was for her own benefit and the family's honor. To prevent her from being promiscuous and ruining her reputation.

Now, her mother stood before her once more, thinking she was doing what was best for her daughter. Farha couldn't stand to look at her. Completely exhausted from her earlier struggles, she put her head back and surrendered her body to them as they worked on grooming her. She kept thinking that the only thing that belonged to her at that moment was her mind. The idea gave her some comfort. The gentle smell of olive oil, now applied to her long brown hair, filled the room. The women's gossipy voices gradually became muffled. Images blurred. Her vision darkened.

Farha slowly drifted to sleep. And instead of the ceiling, now she saw the sun.

Where am I? She brought her hands up to her face and saw they were not her own. She realized she was in a lucid dream, which was exactly where she preferred to be at the moment. Looking down at her almost-naked body and her now-ancient surroundings, she decided she was in the Pharaonic age and in one of the scariest myths she had read about. She let go and let the dream take control.

The heat was unbearable, which made working on the crops harder than it already was and left her glistening with sweat. In the dream, Farha was too distracted with the task to feel uneasy about the king's soldiers, who were dressed in the official Pharaonic headpieces and uniforms, wandering about the homes and lands of the peasants all day. She had just assumed they were giving new orders and so had dismissed the matter entirely up until the moment when she glanced up only to notice that one of the soldiers was staring at her from the edge of the field. As she did so, he saw her face up close for the first time and raised his eyebrows in astonishment, which was a reaction she was used to because her colored eyes were considered very rare, especially blue ones. When he gestured for Farha to continue working, she complied, feeling suspicious and uneasy. She sensed her every movement was being carefully monitored, which made it even harder to plow under the unforgiving Egyptian sun. A few minutes later, the guard came over to where she was squatting and asked her to stand up.

"Do you have parents?" he asked.

Dream Farha gestured towards her home.

He took off in the direction of her house.

Her heartbeat soared, her lips quivered, sweat droplets fell from her forehead. She wondered if she had done something wrong.

She sat on a nearby boulder, waiting for the soldier to leave her house, too afraid to enter while he was there. It only took him a short time to finally head back to where he came from, and she looked gratefully at the growing distance between them. When Farha went inside, the air was thick with tension and she could see a strange expression in the eyes of both her mother and father.

With a shaky voice, she said, "What's wrong?"

Then her father, replying in an unnaturally steady tone said, "This season, you are to be the bride of the Nile."

She had heard and seen it happen to other girls, but somehow never imagined it would be her turn. Her legs didn't feel like they could support her, so she leaned on the wall and asked the only question that came to mind. "Why me?"

"They will come for you after some time," he said. "You are the one that fate has chosen."

He told her that the guards had said, "Honor and blessings will be bestowed upon your family because of your sacrifice," and had explained that it was their destiny. If her father felt any remorse or pain, he was burying it deep under an icy expression. The deed was done.

Somehow she had started to run so fast that she was already at the edge of the river and didn't know when or how she got there. Her legs buckled underneath her so that she was staring at her own blue-eyed reflection in the clear waters, feeling everything and nothing at all. She asked again, "Why me?" And her reflection told her, "Because you're a beautiful tragedy."

A few moments later, there were footsteps behind her, and she was forcibly taken to the temple for the preparation. Three guards had found her sitting by the Nile as silent as the dead. Two of them grabbed an arm each and the third led the way past many other peasants who saw the spectacle and didn't even so much as flinch. At the entrance to the grand temple, a few women received her. She was bathed in waters that were full of odors so strong and sickeningly sweet, she felt her head spin. This ceremony was one of the most sacred and essential, and every step was performed carefully to the highest standards. The Nile had to be pleased with his virgin sacrifice for this ceremony to work. Every single woman present had a role to play. Except her. She was just the sacrifice.

At the exact moment when the sun was starting to descend into the horizon, Farha was standing at the top of the highest rocky mountain with hands and legs bound with a smooth luxurious cloth, the likes of which she had never so much as touched in her lifetime but would die bound by. She could hear the excited cheers coming from the crowd that had gathered to watch the ceremony. In return, the Nile would give them healthy crops for a very long time. The hairs from the expensive wig placed on her head fluttered momentarily, masking her vision, and she was sure her elaborate eyeliner was being ruined by her tears.

They had carefully prepared their offering for this moment. Finally, she was pushed. She didn't even know exactly by whom, but did it matter? In reality, every single one of the spectators had contributed to her demise. As she fell, she saw her curse of a reflection one last time before the splash.

---·◆◆◆◆◆◆·---

Farha was suddenly aware that her face was wet with cold water, real water, and opened her eyes. Her mother had splashed water onto her face to wake her up and prepare her properly for the wedding. The dream was over and she was awake once more … but was there even a difference between the two?

They offered Farha more food. She politely declined, but sneaked two loaves of *baladi* bread into the folds of her *galabeya* when no one was paying attention.

"I'm not feeling well. May I lie down for a few minutes?" she said, and they happily obliged, because, after all, she had finally come to her senses.

Farha, now fueled by adrenaline, stole a few bills that her parents had stashed under their mattress.

She dismissed a passing sense of love for the only people and places that she could call home, especially Ahmed and all the love she had for him. But there was nothing else she could do. Her back was against the wall. Maybe one day she would come back for him.

Without looking back, she climbed through the large hole that was the window, one leg after the other, and landed with a faint thud onto the sandy ground. In her soul, she longed for nothing more than a life that was free. A picture of a bustling city, alive and beating like a living heart, rose up to the forefront of her thoughts. It was a place where all the movies she had seen as a child had a good ending, which was all she ever wanted. It was also the place where Mrs. Soha, the only person who had truly believed in her, lived. Yes, this was her only escape. In her head, she only had one simple plan. Reach Cairo and have the possibility of possibilities.

She was not going to be a falsified myth. She was going to be the reality that her favorite history book had told her about. She was going to be like her early ancestors. Women who were free.

Walaa

In a parallel universe, her 'no' would be an end to her suffering and not the beginning of her end.

She heard a woman scream and sprang up in her bed immediately. She sat up and looked around her bedroom, trying to find the source of the noise. There was no woman. She was the one who had been screaming.

Slowly, Walaa started to be more aware of herself and her surroundings. She was drenched in sweat, and her chest was heaving from the effort of recovering from the adrenaline coursing through her body.

It was a nightmare. The same nightmare she had been having for months. The blade. The man charging forward. The scream. The blood.

Her mother burst into her room. "Walaa, what's wrong?! What's wrong?!"

It was the middle of the night, and her mother, eyes swollen with sleep, came closer.

"I'm fine, Mama. Go back to sleep."

Walaa's frail attempt to reassure her mother and calm her down were in vain.

"Are you still having the same dream?"

In an attempt to not lie, Walaa looked away. Even if she wanted to, she couldn't. Her mother could always tell.

"Is the psychologist not helping?"

Walaa took a deep breath and looked at her mother. "I swear I'm fine. I haven't had that dream in a while. I'm making progress with her, I promise."

Her mother sat down on the bed and hugged her tightly.

After what seemed like a long time, her mother loosened her embrace. "You're shivering, *habibty*." Then, as she always did in moments like these, she asked her daughter to lie down and recited Qur'anic verses in gentle whispers. "Close your eyes, *habibty*. Let me relax you."

And Walaa did. For a long time.

"It's dawn. Let's pray."

After prayers, Walaa faked a smile in an attempt to assure her mother that she felt better.

"Get some sleep, Mama."

"You sure you're okay?"

"Yes, all good," she said and kissed her mother's hand.

But Walaa wasn't okay. She hadn't been in almost a year. At times like these, she got up and wrote a letter to her best friend. She grabbed her bright blue eyeglasses, her favorite color since birth, from the nightstand, put them on, and tied up her very matted curly hair with an overly-stretched hair tie. She got out her notebook from the drawer and began to write.

Dear Amira,

Do you remember when I used to panic before every single exam and how you had to make me human enough to function? I would always obsessively revise until you had to physically grab the book from me and make me stop, then you'd calm me down enough to start making fun of me. I would shout at you, but I'd always end up laughing. You knew just how to fix me, every time. In every situation. Without fail. You were always my backbone when I didn't have one. Remember that time on the metro when a woman cut a strand of my hair because I wasn't wearing a hijab? Till this day I wonder where you got the bravery to curse her like you did. She was triple your size. You were always so brave. So much braver than I could ever be. The day you left me, I don't know what I could have done to stop him, but I'm sorry I wasn't brave enough anyway. I'm just so sorry. Soon, it would have been our eleventh year of being friends. They told me that eventually grief turns into acceptance, but I still miss you. I miss you now more than ever.

Walaa waited for the tears to come, but they didn't. Somehow, that was worse.

She put her notebook back in the drawer and lay back in bed. She didn't know how long she had been like that, staring at the light rectangles dancing on the ceiling, reflections from the gaps between her shutters, when eventually her father walked in.

"Have you had breakfast yet?" he said, looking around at her room as if studying its state of disarray.

"No," she said, dismayed that he was annoyed earlier than usual this time.

"Are you going to stay in bed forever? Are you not going to do something with your life?"

Walaa didn't reply until he walked over to the window and opened the shutters.

Walaa sat up immediately. "Baba, no. Not today!"

"Are you going to hide from the world forever?"

"Just not today, please."

"You say that every day. You're twenty-three, so you need to experience life!"

"I'm doing courses online like you asked me to!"

He sighed. "That's not living life."

"Can you not pressure me please?"

Her father stormed out of her room, stomping all the way until the sound of his footsteps faded away. She wished he appreciated her efforts more. She had enrolled in online translation courses to please him. But going to university was not for her anymore, not after Amira was gone. After it had happened, she just felt out of place, like a weed pretending it was going to flower. And she knew she wasn't going to flower. She didn't relate to anyone around her. They were all too excited and too chatty. She didn't have the energy for that. Plus, if she did talk to them, what would she talk about? Her dead best friend?

But she didn't feel angry at her father though. She felt bad for him, because she knew exactly why he acted that way. He felt devastated that he couldn't help his daughter feel better, so his sorrow turned to anger. She understood that, but she wished she wasn't on the receiving end of his anger so often.

She rested her head on the pillow once more and, soon enough, fell asleep. She didn't know how much time she had been avoiding being alive before she heard her mother barge into her room once more.

"Your appointment is in an hour. Get up and get dressed."

"I'm too tired to go today. Can you cancel it please?"

"Walaa, get up. You can't do this all the time. The psychologist insisted you have to be regular."

"I have a headache. I'll go next time, I promise."

Her mother looked too exhausted to argue, and walked away without another word.

But Walaa felt there was no point in going. That was what she truly felt but could never say to her parents and crush their hopes. Every time she went, the psychologist would say the same thing. That she had PTSD and that she needed coping mechanisms. Then she would drone on and on about tactics to avoid panic attacks. The five senses, she said. Over and over. List something for each sense when you're panicking, she said. The five senses, the five senses, the five senses. Did she not understand what Walaa went through with those five senses? See a man charging towards her best friend and stick a blade into her, just for refusing to marry him. Did *she* see the life leave Amira's eyes as she died? Did *she* have to read comments on online news outlets of people saying Amira deserved it since she wasn't wearing a *hijab*? Or that she would go to Hell for it? Her murdered friend. Her murdered friend was the one going to Hell. Walaa's eyes could so easily remember all the comments justifying her death like a videotape that wouldn't stop. Saying she seduced him, that she must have led him on. Her ears had heard interviews of his neighbors saying he was a good man. That her best friend must have driven him crazy. Did the psychologist go through any of that? All her five senses did was make her hear her best friend scream, smell the metallic blood gushing out of her stomach, touch her face for the last time, see those comments over and over again, and have to swallow the bitter taste of unquenchable rage every time. Those were the five senses to her.

Even as Walaa was lying in bed, just thinking about the outside made her breathing quicken, and if she imagined it more, she would hyperventilate until she had a panic attack. To get through the day, Walaa had to act like the world outside was a place that didn't exist. She was safe in her house. Even safer in her room. This is where she intended to stay. For how long? She didn't know.

Her parents and even her friends didn't understand how dark it was in her head after it happened. But how could they? They weren't there. They weren't there when the man had stalked Amira for months. They weren't there when Amira had filed a police report against him, but no one took her seriously. They weren't there when he threatened to blackmail her by doctoring naked pictures of her. They weren't there when despite Amira constantly telling him to leave her alone, he went to her house to meet with her parents and ask for her hand in marriage. They weren't there when they turned him away. They weren't there when he drove a knife into her body. They weren't there when Walaa saw Amira's parents sob, barely able to hold onto each other for support. They just weren't there. But she was. She was there. And now that's what the outside world was to her in her head. A place where women could be killed just for saying *no*.

Walaa's mother loved to tell her the killer was found and taken to trial. That he had been given a death sentence, and this should make her heal. Maybe it should have, but it didn't. He deserved to suffer. He deserved to die. But Amira didn't. She didn't deserve to die just for saying *no*. None of the women who had similar deaths did. None of the parents that had to mourn their daughters deserved to live with that pain. But that didn't stop her mother from going on and on about the "justice" of it all.

As if on command, her mother walked in again. This time, armed with a tray of food.

"Eat."

"I'm not hungry now."

"Then just have a bite. Please."

Walaa groaned and took the tray.

"So, Tante Yosreya invited us to dinner today."

Walaa knew what was coming, so she didn't reply.

"She really wants you to come. What do you think? You haven't attended a family dinner in a long time."

"I attend family dinners when they are at our house."

"And is that going to go on forever?"

"As long as the world continues to be horrible."

"Not everything about the world is horrible."

That did it for Walaa. The switch flipped.

"Oh really, Mama? Tell me more about that please. Please tell me why I would be standing with my friend in front of her building when the man that had refused to leave her alone for months appears out of nowhere and stabs her? Huh? Why? Is this a wonderful world to you?"

"The world isn't all bad, Walaa. He was."

"Well, millions of him exist. She wasn't the first or the last woman to get killed for refusing a man."

She looked down to calm herself down. Then she heard a strange sound. Sniffles. She looked at her mother, who was crying.

Walaa put the tray down on the nightstand and rushed over to her mother and held onto her arm. "Oh, my God, Mama. I'm… I'm so sorry. I'm so, so sorry. Don't cry."

It was the first time in ages that she had seen her mother falling apart this way.

"You don't even understand how much it hurts to see you go through this. It kills me. It kills me to see how much this has changed you. It kills me that I don't know how to help you. You are my little girl! Every day you mourn her loss, I feel like I mourn you, too."

Through her own tears, Walaa tried to speak but couldn't.

"I don't want to lose you … I … I can't lose you! Please stop being so distant. Let us in."

They both cried as they hugged each other as tightly as two people can.

"I know I left you too that day. I'm sorry. This world scares me without her."

"I know. I don't tell you this, but it scares me too. What makes it easier is that we have each other. You need to be brave. You need to be brave for her. She'd be so sad to see that you've lost your spark."

"I don't know if I can do this. Being around strangers terrifies me now … and the outside—"

"I know you can do it."

"How do you know?"

"Because I know my daughter well. She's still in there"

They held onto each other, both falling apart but being a steadying presence for one another somehow.

"Also, Mama, I need to be honest."

Her mother broke away from the hug, concerned.

"I don't want to go because I really don't want to hear Aunt Yosreya talk about Mohanad from that Turkish series again."

Hearing her mother laugh was the best feeling in the world.

———·◆◆ ◆ ◆◆·———

Five months later, Walaa was walking down a street, in the outside world. Even though she was aware of everyone around her, she didn't shiver anymore. *Turns out when you take therapy seriously, it helps sometimes.* Walaa had been following very careful and slow steps towards feeling better. Today was a brand new step. A big one this time.

The street was less busy than usual. The smell of Turkish coffee wafted towards her from a nearby *qahwa*, together with the familiar sound of hookahs being smoked.

"Hey, honey! Where are you going?"

Walaa turned to look at the source of the noise and, unsurprisingly, found that it was a young man looking at her from across the street.

"Shame on you, son! Walk away before I beat you to your senses."

The harasser laughed. "No need to, *hagg*."

Walaa could see through the harasser. He was scared, she knew. She looked at the old man sitting in the *qahwa* and nodded slightly in a way that said, "Thank you."

He nodded back.

She was shaken. But she was not going to stop, because her best friend wouldn't have wanted her to stop.

Today, her challenge for herself was an even more crowded space than the streets she had been forcing herself to brave. It was the most crowded place possible. Public transportation.

Walaa walked on. Head held high. Was she going to make it? She didn't know. But she was going to try anyway.

Laila

In a parallel universe, her wild soul would entrance him and make him desire her as his exhilarating forever, and not leave her abandoned, unloved, unwanted.

She stood at the edge of the glistening Ras Sedr Sea, jeans almost touching the salt water. She was finally here. After many years and inner battles, she could make herself come here again.

Last time Laila was here, her mother was with her. Now, she had to make peace with the fact that she had to be here without her.

She hadn't gotten to spend much time with her mother, and yet, she was the person who had impacted her the most in life. From time to time, no matter how many years had passed, she would remember random details about her. At the funeral, many people told her this would happen. She remembered things like how her mother loved listening to Edith Piaf. *Yes.* She remembered, because of that time she grabbed her hand when a song by her came on the radio and they started to spontaneously dance in the kitchen; they twirled and twirled until happiness and dizziness were all her eleven-year-old body could feel. Her mother was a warrior, and the warmth of the sun intertwined. She was the kind of person who always managed to make moments feel special, no matter how ordinary they were, with her laughter, jokes, hugs, or mere presence. Her smile never wavered even at the end of her days, when Laila was seventeen. Her illness was slow, cruel, relentless.

Laila had known cancer to be an expert killer, even before it even touched their lives. Watching it unfold right in front of her was something else. She now knew the depth to which it could turn one's own body against itself. Making the body's own cells its destruction, as if cancer knows the thing most capable of destroying a person is themselves.

As she stood at the edge of the water, Laila instinctively reached for her necklace, something she had done for many years without ever realizing it. She remembered the day her mother had given it to her. The memory was a little fuzzy, yet permanently preserved, like an echo running through her veins, back and forth, never ending.

Laila had stood next to the door for her usual get-it-together moment before going in to see her mother again. It reminded her of the swimming lessons she used to take as a child. *Take a deep breath, dive. Take a deep breath, dive.* She could not withstand another goodbye moment wearing a disguise. This time, it was a little different, though, as her mother had something physical to give her.

"This belonged to my grandmother," her mother said. "It was passed down in our family, and I want to give it to you."

Laila swallowed hard and held the necklace like it was a treasure that had been lost at sea and sought out for centuries. Never in her life had she seen something so delicate. It was a thin gold necklace with a small pendant made of natural pearls. Her eyes watered, but luckily her thoughts were interrupted by her mother's touch, jolting her out of drowning in the feeling.

They looked into each other's eyes for a moment, and then her mother said, "Now what is the most precious thing you own?"

Without missing a beat, Laila responded, "This! I will take very good care of it, Mama, don't worry." And, as if to reassure her, Laila clutched the tiny pendant even tighter.

Her mother smiled kindly, the little dimple on her left cheek making a now rare appearance. She was going to miss that dimple. "The most precious thing you will always have is time. You will have far more expensive and beautiful things than this necklace, but nothing compares to time. It's the only thing you have that you can never lock away in a closet or save for your future children. You never know how much you will have of it left; all you will ever know is that it is moving fast. There is really only one thing you can do with time and that is to use it. Use every bit of it in a way that makes it even more precious."

When her mother was gone, Laila had made it her life's purpose to follow her advice, and standing at the edge of the sea, this was one of those times. That piece of advice governed her actions and made life worth living for her. She treasured her years as much as she did her minutes, and she tried to make as many of her moments as meaningful as she could.

At this moment, standing in front of the waves that continued to whisper to her, she missed plunging into the sea, with every part of her being. Her desire to do so overcame the logic telling her not to go in for a swim in jeans and a T-shirt. It called to her. She waded in, jeans becoming uncomfortably heavy with water, but feeling a surge of happiness as she took the plunge. Cold water. A rush. Maybe someday she would understand why God had to make a beautiful soul like her mother suffer so much. *Maybe.* But for now, she floated on the soft, comforting blanket of the Red Sea, immersed in a world of silvery blue. A moment that was a little sad but also magical.

Emerging out of the water, however, was a less beautiful experience, and her body began to shiver when touched by the cool early morning air. That was what almost always happened after these "let me create a beautiful moment for myself" decisions: she would end up feeling stupid, but she knew that these "I'm an idiot" thoughts didn't last very long. She would look back at this moment when it became a memory and feel warm.

Now, though, she wished she had a towel, a blanket, anything. Anything to make the sting of cold disappear. She walked, shivering, towards the outdated yet charming hotel she knew so well, laughing at the sight of a golden retriever playfully tackling his owner.

"Laila?"

She turned around. It was the tackled-by-a-golden-retriever man.

The dog ran towards her as if her name was the "go" signal. Laila bent down to greet him. He was so fluffy and warm, she wanted to melt into his fur for a heavy dose of serotonin. She looked up warily at the stranger walking towards them.

"I'm sorry if I scared you. I'm just sure I know you. Did you take tennis lessons at Heliopolis Club when you were younger?"

"Yes?" Her brows automatically furrowed.

"Oh, my God, you're shivering. One second." He jogged awkwardly to his umbrella and came back with a towel.

She took it and thanked him. He looked relieved when she did.

The dog wouldn't stop cutely pestering her for more pats. "What's his name?"

"Caramella"

"Oh, it's a girl?"

"Well, no…my sister named him years ago. Don't offend him, he's very insecure about his name."

She laughed in spite of herself. "And are you going to tell me who you are, or—"

"Oh, I'm so sorry!" He held out his hand and she took it. "Ali. We used to be on the same kids' tennis team. You were very nice to me, even though I was a really quiet kid and kind of left out."

"Wait, I remember you. What a strange coincidence—"

"Yes, I thought I recognized you when you walked into the sea, but then you … swam with your clothes on. I got a little worried, to be honest."

She snorted with laughter as she imagined what she had just done as seen through the eyes of a stranger.

"I swear I don't mean to intrude, but I'm just so curious … why?"

"It's okay. You're the reason I'm not Squizz ice cream right now, so you may ask," she joked.

He got so visibly excited, it was adorable. "That was my favorite ice cream growing up! I used to get it right after practice."

"A man with taste I see."

His phone rang. A Metallica song.

"I take it back. Very clichéd taste."

He laughed, revealing a dimple on his right cheek that reminded her of her mother's, and showed Laila his screen. It read *Big Bad Boss*.

Laila laughed too; for some reason, she found herself letting her guard down.

"So, tell me, why the random sea bath?"

"I think you're looking for a logical explanation, like I was covered in ants or something."

"Very logical."

Why was he making me laugh so easily? All I know is his name, and his taste in music.

"Okay are you ready?"

He nodded and dramatically straightened up.

"So before my mother died, she told me to make use of every moment in life and make it mean something and all that social media quote stuff."

"Okaaay ... we can go back to ants if you'd like," he said awkwardly.

"No, it's totally okay. That was years ago."

"Yes, but I don't think that ever stops hurting."

"Now you're just trying to make me sad on purpose," she teased.

"No, no, I'm sorry. I just mean ... I lost my dad a year ago, so I can sort of understand where you're coming from."

She noticed that at some point they had naturally sat down next to each other on the sand to talk.

"Were you close to him?" she asked gently, feeling that they had gone miles and broken barriers by sheer coincidence.

"Not that much, maybe when I was younger. Some fathers are hard on their sons for some reason. My friends say that about theirs, too. I'm closer to my mother, I guess. What about you and your father?"

"Oh, we're very close, even closer when my mom passed away. He's my best friend."

The sun was starting to rise. The sky was in shades of pastel colors, the colors that don't scream beautiful, but whisper it.

Yes, her mother's words were always right. The unlikely decision she had taken could lead to special moments like this.

Laila had always felt that even though some moments seemed entirely ordinary, there was always something special to notice, like how, when the sun met his eyes, they were no longer brown, but molten gold swimming in chocolate. She couldn't look away.

They sat talking for two more hours.

The way there was instant chemistry, there was an almost instant start to a relationship. It only took him a few weeks to say he loved her, and it only took a second for her to say she did too.

He always knew what to say and when to say it. She had never let herself have feelings for anyone. Not once in her twenty-five years of being on this earth. Losing one more person in her life would have been too much for her to handle.

But with him, she let herself fall, because she believed in him like it was the most natural thing in the world.

Of course he had his issues, but didn't everyone? She knew enough from being her friends' relationship therapist that issues were a natural part of being in any relationship.

She noticed that the stress from his job was one of his main triggers. He couldn't handle it. It consumed him, and he often told her he hated it more than anything else in the world.

Mixed in with his sweet words and sweeter gestures, there were sprinkles of anger. Their fights were often explosive. He tended to lose his temper, and almost become someone else, someone she didn't recognize. But then he would apologize, and she knew he was genuine about it, and they would go right back to heaven itself. For her, the beauty of their relationship far outweighed the issues they had, because no one had ever made her more comfortable than he did. He was her best friend. She could tell him anything in the world and he wouldn't judge her. Every night, she couldn't wait to call him and tell him all about her day and listen to his. He was a future to look forward to no matter how dark life got sometimes. Being with him kept her going. They both worked on themselves, him on becoming less triggered, and her on being less triggering for him.

Ali could make anything funny. No one made her laugh as much as he did. No one. He could even transform pain into a comedy. When asked about what he did for a living he would always say, "I work in finance in a multinational. A multinational pain in the ass."

Laila, however, could always see beyond the humor, right into the pain.

One Friday morning, while they sat in their favorite cafe, she decided to make a risky move and talk to him about it.

"Okay, how about you go back to what you love? Maybe go back to architecture."

"That means starting over, and I'm at a good point in my career."

"We can always start over. I'll be here by your side. We can do it together."

"It's not that easy, not everything is as dreamlike as you say it is. Not everything is fixable."

"I never said it was easy. I just don't want you to spend the rest of your life doing something that makes you so unhappy."

"Laila, can you stop pushing all the time? It's exhausting. Can we change the subject? We don't have to talk about difficult topics all the time."

"How is this a difficult topic, Ali? I don't understand."

"It is for me. You do this all the time. It's exhausting for me."

"Okay, sorry. I'll stop."

She felt hurt. She was just trying to help and didn't think the topic was hurtful. She just wanted him to be healthier and happier. *But everyone has their boundaries right? Maybe I just need to stop pushing so he's happy. Maybe I'm the problem..*

"Here are some lovely words of advice from the wisest man I know," she said, trying to sound positive to lift his mood, hiding how she truly felt

"That would be me of course."

"That's the funniest thing you've said all day."

He laughed. "What does the *hagg* say?"

"He always says 'get a job for food and a hobby for mood.' Maybe you just need to plan your time better so you have more time for the food and the mood together. Plus, I will always, always be here for you. You're never alone, Ali. We will get through everything together, I promise."

She held out her hand and he took it.

"I love your father. Can't wait to be part of your family someday."

He hugged her. She felt safe. Happy tears filled her eyes for the first time since forever.

Bliss.

If only words were enough.
If only people did what they said they would.
If only actions and words were married for eternity
But in reality, they weren't.
Oh, reality. When will you stop being so painful?

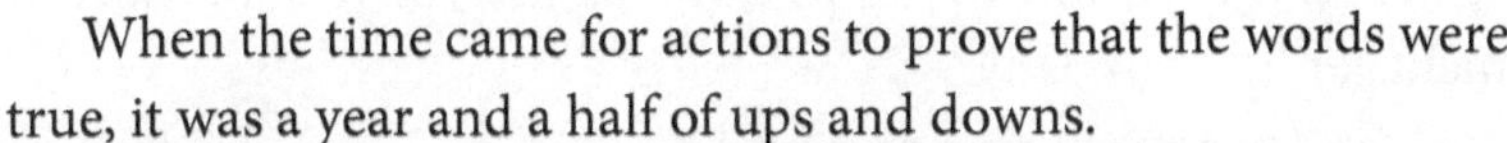

When the time came for actions to prove that the words were true, it was a year and a half of ups and downs.

Even though Laila was not a get-married-immediately person and believed she needed to know the person first, she began to feel that it was time for at least a window into serious commitment, and she couldn't wait for her father to meet him. It was usually just her talking about an image of their future together, united in a home, their own version of family. When she voiced these concerns, he seemed to concur, and she was satisfied.

A few weeks later, Laila sat in a café, smiling from ear to ear, opposite Ali's mother, Tant Hanaa, who had asked to meet Laila before Ali met with her father.

She didn't look anything like him, but she felt as though she loved her already.

When they first met, Laila went for the usual kisses on the cheek greeting, but his mother interrupted with a handshake. Laila was a little taken aback, but it was fine. Maybe she wasn't a fan of physical touch.

Next to the mother, Ali smiled, but she knew him enough to know the smile was fake. He looked distant, but he had been this way for a while. Lately, they had gotten into many fights about him pulling away and not spending enough time together. She felt abandoned most of the time, but he had told her it was just a temporary surge in work. He seemed genuine, so she believed him.

"Tante, you don't know how happy I am to finally meet you!"

While both women exchanged pleasantries, Laila couldn't help but notice the mother's eyes slowly traveling from her dyed dark burgundy hair down to her nose piercing.

"I can't wait to get to know you better."

"Sure, darling. May I start?"

"Of course. What would you like to know?"

"Work. Let's begin with that," she started, and turned to look at her son. He didn't look up. "Ali tells me you're some sort of manager in a company."

"Yes, I'm a marketing manager at—"

"Yes. Ali told me."

Laila felt her stomach drop. All the uncomfortable moments that had been happening since the event began came to the forefront of her brain. Ali's mother's tone didn't seem friendly. Something wasn't right.

"But do you think it is wise that a wife should abandon her home responsibilities for work?"

Laila looked at Ali for assistance, but he was looking down at his hands. It was the first time that someone was this blunt with their judgment.

"Ali and I already talked about everything. We both believe that marriage is a partnership, so we would both like to do what we love, finance our lives together, and share home responsibilities since our working hours are the same."

"Share … home responsibilities? How can you expect a man to do housework?"

"I mean, he has two hands like I do, right?"

Laila tried to laugh, but Ali's mother's reaction made her come to an abrupt stop.

"It's natural roles, darling. It's always been this way." Even though she said 'darling', the word was cold as a blade.

"Men don't cook, they don't clean, they don't know how to."

"But, Tante, think about it, they do. There are male cleaners in every establishment and cooks at every restaurant. Men do these jobs. Most only do it when they're getting paid, but they very much have the ability to do these things if they want to. It's just that some take the easier way out and expect their wives to do it for them, regardless of the amount of things that their wives have on their plate. If we both have dreams to achieve, it's only fair; I'm sure you can see that."

Again, Laila attempted to lock eyes with Ali, but he avoided her gaze. *Why was he not saying anything? They had talked about all of this since day one, what was happening?*

The one-sided war of questions went on for a while. And still, Ali didn't meet her eyes.

After many fights over that day, and many times of Ali assuring her that he would deal with his mother and that she wouldn't meddle in their lives, the storm passed.

Laila wanted to believe more than anything that things were okay, but a part of her felt that they weren't. She dismissed the feeling because, after all, he had promised her the world, hadn't he?

About a month later, she and Ali got into a silly argument while texting. She knew from experience that text fights were bound to make things worse than they actually were, so she called him.

"Ali, can we just—"

"Laila, I don't want to be in this relationship anymore."

Her disbelief was louder than the silence that stretched between them. *There was no way this was actually happening.*

"I don't understand…!"

"I want to end this."

"Ali, what … what are you saying? Whatever it is you're upset about, we can fix it. We can fix it. I can work on anything you want. I can change." Her breath quickened, her heart was racing, her vision blurred. She felt dizzy and disconnected from everything.

"Laila, don't."

"Please. What did I do? Just tell me …where is this coming from, what's happening? I'm so confused."

"Just stop."

"Wait, just … wait, ok? Is it because of what happened with your mother?"

"No, I agree with her beliefs. I always have."

"I don't understand. I told you what I believed from day one. You never said anything. You never disagreed. Can we just at least meet and talk face to face? Can we not end years of being together over the phone? You're my best friend. Please."

"Laila…" He paused. "I don't love you anymore. I don't want to marry you."

A few seconds later, they both hung up.

A sound escaped Laila's lips. It was a cross between crying and screaming.

She couldn't stand up anymore. She sat on the carpeted floor of her bedroom. She tried to scream into her hands so her father wouldn't hear. Her muffled screams wouldn't stop. Her body was shaking, her heart beating so fast, she felt like it would never slow down. Agonizing pain.

At some point, her father came up from behind her. She collapsed sobbing into his arms.

That night, Laila screamed and cried while her father tried to make her feel better, but couldn't. She could see the pain in his eyes as he watched his daughter scream with pain, but she couldn't care and couldn't stop herself. She felt as though her world had collapsed in on itself. She couldn't make sense of what had happened and felt like throwing up.

What does the world mean if he isn't in it?

Screams of "I want to die" escaped her lips without her realizing. Over and over again, like a prayer.

Her father only held onto her tighter. When her sobbing wouldn't stop, he gave her the sleeping pills he had been taking every night since her mother's passing.

Hours later, Laila's crying stopped.

That night, they lay in each other's arms, two souls who had lost the people who meant everything to them.

Laila sat at her therapist's office. She had been going there since her mother's passing.

"How? Why? He … always said he loved me. He told me he wanted to marry me a few weeks ago. He always acted like he did. Why did he do it? I don't understand anything. I thought we were doing so well."

"I can never know for sure. No one can, but I don't believe he stopped loving you so suddenly. It doesn't work that way. He probably told you the only thing he knew you could not offer to work on or suggest to fix."

"What do you mean?" she asked, suppressing sobs.

"You give all of you into everything in your life, all your energy. He's smart. He knows that. If he had said it was about him needing time, you would wait, you would work on it. His mother, you would have made peace with her even if she hurt you. He knows you would have done anything to make it work, but if he said he doesn't love you, there is nothing you can do about it. He wanted a way to run."

"But … how … why? He just gave me a necklace engraved with my mother's name. He recently told me he wanted to be part of my family."

"Did he ever actually do something, take actions that showed you he wanted to get married?"

"We always talked about our plans for the future."

"Think back. Was he planning with you, or was he going along with it?"

"He brought his mother to meet me."

"Did he suggest it, or was he just going along with it? Did he actually plan anything, Laila? His own future? Did he know what he wanted in life? Or what he wanted to achieve? Was he ever motivated enough to take a step towards anything? Did he have the courage?"

"No."

"He is a person who lives in fear, Laila. But you, you are bravery itself."

Months passed like sandpaper scraping her heart.

Something inside her had changed. She didn't want to be close to anyone ever again. She distanced herself from all her friends. She had been too innocent. She now knew that people didn't always mean what they say. *What a bitter lesson to learn. How stupid could I be?*

Since the breakup, it all came back to her slowly, like a file being downloaded on very slow Wi-Fi.

He really was nothing more than words. Words. Beautiful words.. Words that couldn't have been said in a better way or at a better time. Wise words. Words that understood her soul.

But that didn't change what they always were and always would be.

Words.

And words don't make a life.

Maybe she had been blind. Maybe he hadn't accepted all of her. Maybe he had wanted to. Maybe he had just said what she wanted to hear. Maybe he had just liked the idea of her. A woman who saw him as wonderful and painted a picture of his potential for his own eyes to see. Maybe he had just liked the reflection of himself in her eyes, the acceptance and the compassion that he didn't have for himself, but not the wild soul behind them.

Ever since the breakup, the world wasn't the same anymore, or was it she who didn't see the world the same? She didn't know. It was darker, scarier.

Some days were made of realizations, some were made of hours of tears. Some were even made of desperation and the desire to reach out to him even if it meant that she would lose her dignity. But the constant factor was the heartache that continued to exist like a parasite under her skin.

Years before, she had learned to mourn a deceased loved one. Now she had to learn to mourn someone who was alive and had chosen to abandon her. By choice.

On a random sunny morning, leaving her therapist's office, she couldn't stand to be with her own self, her own thoughts, her own existence anymore. She had to be somewhere where the voices around her were louder than those inside her.

She took slow, deliberate steps towards the nearest metro station.

Dalia

In a parallel universe, her dreams would be a source of bountiful pride, and not a cry for battle.

She had always been known amongst all who knew her as that rare breed of human, a morning person. Her many, many friends knew and so often joked about the bursting bundle of energy that she was, and so did her family. That was the kind of person Dalia was. Always surrounded by people and being the life of any gathering. It was second nature to her existence since birth. After all, when you're born a twin to the first male child in a family, one has to create an edge for themselves. Dalia's chosen methods to garner any form of attention to herself were to overachieve and to be bubbly, and so it had been ever since.

That morning was no different. When the birds began to sing, she was awake. In her small, but sophisticatedly decorated bedroom, she quickly got up, opened the shutters, and took a minute to take in the sight of the slowly growing Cairo traffic five floors down. She performed all her usual morning routines with practiced ease, and made good time. She even had time for a quick run on the treadmill and a cold shower. After a healthy breakfast consisting of her putting fruit on almost everything, and after carefully choosing her work outfit, a white blazer with a white *hijab* to match, paired with her favorite maxi skirt, she flew off.

Standing in the crowded metro is a nuisance to anyone living in Cairo, but since she had to use it every single day, she had decided to befriend it. As soon as she got onto the metro, she would put her headphones on and listen to her favorite podcast about success and motivation, and following that, would often hold a brainstorming session for work conducted between the different thoughts in her head.

As she reached the artery-thin Zamalek street in which she worked, she was greeted by her favorite office errands worker, *Am* Amin, who always treated her like a daughter, and was probably on his way to grab something that had run out from the office kitchen.

"You're a little early today, Miss Dalia."

"Oh, you know me, *Am* Amin, always so much work to get to."

"Of course I know you! It's been four years, not a couple of days!

"Am I sensing that you're bored of me, *Am* Amin?"

"Oh, never, Miss Dalia. You make the day brighter!"

After the two exchanged a few more pleasantries, Dalia headed over to Strive, the PR agency in which she had spent the bulk of the last few years of her life, and where she had relentlessly fought to reach a top position.

Most people assumed Dalia's life and career were easy. Many of those she worked with openly disliked her and did everything in their power to stunt her career growth. After all, to them, she was a young, dangerously ambitious woman trying to reach the top of a ladder she was never even supposed to glimpse. It wasn't easy in a male-dominated hierarchy to rise as a woman, and this was made even harder because of her *hijab*, which some people perceived as incommensurate with strength, drive, and the desire to succeed. But to Dalia, that was a challenge she was determined to overcome, and she had worked tirelessly, balancing university and work to get a head start. And she had pulled it off, having already made strides in her career by the time she graduated.

The ancient elevator door pinged, signaling her arrival to Floor 9. The cool, familiar glass doors pushed back against her hand as she entered. This. This was where she thrived. Where she came into her own.

Almost no one had made it to the office yet. She was running in a different time zone after all. She was on HR contract time, and everyone else was on working-in-Egypt time. That is everyone, except Marwan. He, on the other hand, was always on competing-with-Dalia time, 24/7, all year long.

"Look who it is! Morning, Doudou!"

"Ah! Marwan, how was your weekend?"

"Well I didn't get much relaxation time. You know how Mr. Adham has been handing me more projects lately. I barely have time for anything."

"You're not alone. Weekends from weekdays are all the same to me."

"I can see that. You look a bit tired. It shows in your eyes," he said with a look of fake compassion. "Don't let work steal your youth like that. I'm sure down the road, you'll regret it."

Dalia opened her mouth to reply to this almost daily passive-aggressive attitude, but was interrupted by Engy, her work bestie.

"Good morning, Marwan," she said. "Dalia! I have a new update on the brief to tell you. Come make coffee with me."

"Brief?" he said. "You ladies make sure to tell me that fresh piece of gossip later, all right?"

Engy brought out her fakest laugh as she grabbed Dalia's shoulder to take her away.

As they walked away, they heard, "Engy, I like your blouse by the way. A little dressed up today, aren't we? Do you have a date or something?"

A few steps away, Dalia turned to Engy. "You need to report his constant comments about your clothing and the way he looks at you to HR. He won't stop otherwise."

"And say what?" replied Engy. "He will say he didn't mean anything by it and that they were innocent comments. He always makes sure to word it in a way that could be perceived as unintentional. It will be my word against his."

"Yes, but surely –"

"Let it go! I've missed you! Let's catch up over a cup of coffee before you get into your work mode."

As the day went on, Dalia managed to finish her tasks way ahead of her usual schedule, which left her feeling satisfied. But it also meant she had more time to just be with her thoughts. Busy was the state she preferred to exist in, and busy was what she had been ever since she could remember. Placed on her desk were memorabilia to prove it. There in the center was the picture of her on graduation day, wearing her highest honors sash – and right next to it, a picture of her winning a basketball tournament as a teenager. To the left, her work achievements, the yearly awards and honorary certificates. But her favourites were the tiny gifts and sticky notes from colleagues across the years. Mostly, they were thank you notes addressed to her for helping them out of a situation whether work-related or personal. A helper, a wall to lean on, a person to depend on. Those were all synonymous with Dalia in people's heads. She couldn't really remember a time when she was the one being helped. She couldn't remember opening up at all.

As the work day drew to a close, people started to get up and leave. She felt tired. Her stomach grumbled as loud as a car driven by a young man trying to show off, and she had to glance back to make sure no one had heard it. Luckily, two of her favorite coworkers approached her.

"We're going to that new Lebanese place across the street. Come with us," said a visibly more exhausted Engy than the one that had dragged her away from Marwan that morning.

"Great! I'm starving. Let me just grab my blazer."

As soon as they walked into the Lebanese place, Dalia relaxed. She'd always found it pleasant; it was simply decorated, mostly painted off-white, and with one wall made entirely of glass. It was naturally lit, which was the kind of vibe that always made Dalia relax.

The trio picked an empty table near the entrance. Dalia ordered a *fattoush* salad, and jokes soon filled the air.

"So then, as always, drooling after that promotion, Marwan walked in on the conversation, and almost immediately agreed with Kariman without knowing what was happening and—" said Engy.

"And Kariman told him, 'so you also think ultra-thin pads are a cash grab?'" added Zahraa.

Engy turned to Dalia. "You should have seen him. He mumbled something and walked away. I almost burst trying not to laugh in his face."

Dalia spluttered with laughter. "You know what almost actually burst today? My eye from Lina trying to show me her engagement ring for the fifth time this week. No, seriously, she almost poked my eye out!"

Just then, her phone rang. It was her mother. Rolling her eyes, she excused herself, got up, and walked to the back of the restaurant to take the call.

The customary "Where exactly are you?" greeted her.

She couldn't resist a sarcastic, "I'm at the disco."

Her mother produced her signature sigh of dramatic disapproval. As always, Dalia's sarcasm did not go down well with her mother, so she gave a more serious answer.

"I'm with friends from work."

With this short answer began her mother's usual all-too-long rant. She disapproved of so many things in Dalia's life and didn't hesitate to tell her about it every time she had the chance, as if following a curated checklist from hell.

"I hardly ever see you anymore. You leave so early in the morning and come back saying you're too tired to spend time with me. There are more valuable ways to spend your time."

"I never hear you say that to my brother about *his* work."

Her mother ignored the remark, and the next part of the rant began. Even though Dalia knew it was coming, she could not help but feel her stomach churn.

"Listen to me, Dalia. You're thirty-three years old and you need to think of your future."

Then, to Dalia's dismay, her mother added, "I'm phoning to tell you that Tante Saneya has found a suitor for you. An engineer with a great income. His family lives in a compound in New Cairo, and they are quite well-connected."

"I am not in any way going to marry some guy just because he lives in New Cairo, and especially not someone recommended by Tante Saneya! I keep telling you that *if* I do get married, it would be to someone I choose, so can we please leave this intrusive woman out of my personal life?"

"You are ungrateful and don't know what's good for you. Fine. Find a husband yourself," she said in a hurt tone and hung up.

Dalia sighed in exasperation. As she walked back, a few people were staring curiously at her, looking amused by the snatch of conversation they had overheard. She decided to go out for a breath of fresh air, and pushing the glass restaurant door open, stepped outside.

She couldn't help but dwell on the striking difference between her own plans and desires for her life and those of her mother and the rest of society. To them, 'the clock was ticking and she should be careful not to die an old shrew.' To her, the matter was entirely different. She was happy with where she was in life. She was building a successful career, praised and loved by all her friends – and one or two members of her family – but most of all, she was confident and satisfied with herself. A husband would come when he was meant to, if he was meant to.

Though most people would come to the conclusion that she must be completely undesirable for being unmarried at her age, they didn't know she had almost gotten engaged once. A few years before, when she had acceded to her mother's requests simply to keep the peace, one salon meeting had gone unusually well. There was instant chemistry. The relationship had turned serious very quickly because they seemed to be on the same page about everything. Better still, he was always there for her whenever she needed him, and he treated her like a friend. Everything was galloping along smoothly, until things came to a screeching halt. A few weeks before the engagement party, as they sat sipping coffee at a café, the casual conversation became a memory she would never forget.

"Everything is going great. I finally decided to take your advice and sent the invitation to my boss. He seemed truly flattered. What would I do without my smart, smart girl?"

"You wouldn't make it through one day."

"So what did your boss say when you said you were quitting?"

She tilted her head in confusion. "What?"

"Did you still not tell him you were quitting?"

"Why would I quit?"

"Well, your mother and I had an agreement. I thought that was something you would prefer."

"I never told you that. Why did you think that?"

"I just thought … you'd prefer not to put your career above your future home and children, like most women would do. You wouldn't have the pressure of making a living."

"Isn't this something you should have talked to me about? And, by the way, I don't work just for the money; I actually enjoy it. You know that what I do is very important to me."

He frowned. "Well your mother and I had an agreement. I was clear with her from the start. She told me that it wouldn't be a problem and that she would talk to you about it. I'm guessing she hasn't done so yet."

"I know this seems like a small deal to you, an easy sacrifice, but it isn't for me."

"I understand what you're saying, but I also know how stressful work can be and how time-consuming it is. Wouldn't you prefer a more relaxed life?"

"I'm sure some people do. But not me. Yousef, you know I love my job. Why would you hide something like this from me?"

"To be honest, I thought that when we talked, you would change your mind."

"So you waited until just before the engagement party so I wouldn't be able to say no? That's very manipulative."

There was a lump in her throat, and a tear almost escaped, but she pretended to rub her eyes. She had learned from a young age that people don't respect women who cry. Every time she showed weakness, it was used against her. Both at work and in life. She had vowed to herself that vulnerability was for her and her alone.

"It's not manipulative. I love you, and I want us to be together."

"Even if something is done out of love, it could still be manipulative."

"Call it what you want. The reality of the situation is, this is my preference for my wife."

"But it isn't mine."

Yousef nodded, seemingly in disapproval. He looked away from her, and she did too. Dalia heard the voices of the people chatting around them and the music playing in the cafe fading away. She seemed only to hear what Yousef had just told her—and, worse, her mother and Yousef making decisions about her personal life behind her back. She felt that lump in her throat again.

"So now what?" Yousef said.

"I don't know. I really love you, but I hoped you would like me as I am, that you would want me to be happy and do what I love. Don't you care if I'm happy?"

"Of course I care. But this is what I believe. This is what I want."

"So that's it?"

He sighed. "Unless you change your mind, then yes, sadly, that's it."

Dalia tried to find any form of regret in his eyes, but there was none. She felt her world crumbling. She had always known her mother would do anything to marry her off, but to go that far? Plot behind her back?

"What about my life, Yousef? What about my beliefs? You just can't stand the thought of me making more money than you and the fact that I'm more successful. I see it in your eyes every time I talk about my job, but I thought you were a bigger man than this."

"That's not true. Even if it was, that's only natural. All men are like this."

"I don't think so. Many of my friends work, and they're married."

"Well then, that's just the way I am. Take it or leave it."

And with that, they said their goodbyes and left.

Later that day, she bolted through the door, attempting to reach her room before facing the dreaded conversation with her mother. Just as she thought she had made it, her mother pounced on her.

"And how was the outing for our bride?" she asked, before scanning Dalia's devastated facial expression.

"It's off. The engagement is off. You thought you could make decisions for me behind my back, but you can't."

Then she half-walked, half-ran to the shelter of her room and locked the door. The next few weeks had consisted of an incessant silent treatment from her mother, interrupted only by yelling or pleading.

"Pretend to go along with it and see what you can do later if you care about that job so much," she kept saying. "Be smarter with your man. You can always try to get what you want with a little patience."

But for the life of her, Dalia couldn't understand how her mother was okay with Dalia having to manipulate her own husband into letting her be herself.

After the breakup, Dalia took the bulk of her annual leave days in one go and spent the entire time in bed between crying when no one was there and fighting when her mother wouldn't leave her alone.

———·◆◆ ◆ ◆◆·———

Now, and from where she stood in front of the restaurant, looking at the busy chaotic street, she crossed her arms, slowed down her breathing, and tried to gain perspective. Sometimes, even through her wall of confident composure and confidence, a bullet was able to penetrate.

It was as if everyone around her had a schedule of when they could catch her at her most vulnerable moments and shoot. Their trained mouths aimed careful comments and rude questions about how she wasn't married yet. They were shooters poised in every concealed position in her life. At weddings, family gatherings, work, friends' outings. Even with all the success she had managed to achieve, that seemed to matter the least to the world around her. In their eyes, she was probably the least successful person on the planet; she hadn't managed to acquire a husband even at thirty-three, and the irony of it was, failure was her biggest fear.

All her life, people's idea of a blessing was to wish her that she would soon be a bride, ignoring anything else that she could ever desire. She always thought it funny that the words for bride and doll were the same in Egyptian Arabic. It was as if people were emphasizing the fact that both were the same.

During each milestone of her life, it was always the same thing, whether a graduation cap on her head, a basketball trophy held high, a certificate of achievement in her hands, or a promotion, the words of congratulations always ended with "And we are sure we will see you soon as a beautiful bride." They built her up with only one expectation, and she hadn't managed to achieve it yet, which meant that until then, she would always be regarded as a failure and nothing she could do would make up for it. No matter how much she pretended it wasn't happening, she knew herself enough to realize it was true.

People probably thought that she was emotionless, all about work, that she didn't feel pain, that she was always happy. But what they saw wasn't always the truth. At her age, and being a social person, she had attended more weddings than she could count. And she would dance and sing and laugh and be the girl everyone thought she was and needed her to be. But in quiet moments, at those weddings, when she would look at the bride and groom dancing, she felt unbearable loneliness weighing on her heart. She looked at them holding onto one other and felt like she wanted to be held by someone too. She wanted to be supported. She wanted to be loved. She wanted to let her guard down. But only with someone who was worth it – if such a person existed.

Till then, she could count on her strongest supporter.

The one who hadn't let her down once. Not for a single second. Always consoling her when she hit the ground. Always reminding her of her value and of the plans that they had drawn together from a young age sitting in bed at night, failing to fall asleep, and instead only managing to dream, and dream, and dream. Her best and most powerful supporter had always been herself.

She was the one who celebrated herself when she got a good grade on a test and didn't find the celebration she was looking for in other people. She was the one who managed to pat herself on the back if no one came to a basketball game she played. She was the one who hugged herself ever so tightly when she found out that her school crush liked her best friend, and through the years had taught herself that she was worthy, that she was beautiful, day by day, night by night. Even if everyone left, even if no one believed in her. She would always be there for herself. She was already whole, already enough, already loved by herself.

Still, sometimes she wished people would stop trying to push her to the ground. All those people who compared her life to an ancient checklist that everyone was expected to follow, and never to question. People who only knew how to break. Especially her own mother, whose womb was the first to put her pieces together.

She pulled herself together and took a deep breath to calm herself down and rebuild her composure. With a graceful stride, she rejoined her friends and cracked a good-natured joke about herself, trying to hide any evidence of the war she had always been fighting.

Nour

In a parallel universe, disapproving stares would not be etched onto her skin, her hair, her entire being.

She had spent most of the day submerged in her art and was waking up to reality for the first time in hours. She got up, stretched a little, and walked further and further away from the painting she'd been working on for days and, thankfully, was now almost complete. It amazed her every single time what a few strokes of paint and a little bit of emotion could do to an empty canvas. Her studio, cluttered and chaotic, stood before her. All sorts of color-stained art supplies littered two large wooden tables. In between the tables stood her aisle and canvas. To the left, a large open window told her it was almost sunset and, therefore, that it was time.

In the bathroom, Nour stood scrubbing oil paint off of her hands with turpentine, slowly making peace with the fact that some of it was just not going to go away that day. Then she got dressed in a loose white blouse and a pair of patterned pants to go for her daily sunset walk on the Nile corniche. Before exiting her apartment, she circled back and took a picture of herself in her studio with the golden hour sunlight streaming in through the window and posted the story to her moderately popular art page. Outside the building, she dodged the disapproving glances from the *bawab* sitting on his throne of judgment, condemning her for no reason, she guessed, other than her being a woman living alone. He wasn't even the only one; all her neighbors had made it passive-aggressively clear that they shared his views. But, for some reason, the *bawab* had decided that he was their morality spokesman.

Nour had almost turned the corner and thought she had escaped his back-handed small talk before she was stopped in her tracks.

"Away for your walk again, Miss Nour?"

"Yes, *Am* Sayed," she said, attempting to walk away swiftly.

"Will you be back late again, past midnight?"

"And why are you asking?"

"Oh, you know, Miss Nour, I want to know because I need to lock up the building door before I sleep. And I don't let my daughter lock it up so late at night."

"I have a key, sleep soundly." She mumbled a quick *salamo aleikom* and left him.

Nour had given up trying to be nice to anyone in the building. When her ex-husband had first moved out of the apartment after their divorce, she had seen a shift happening in the neighbors' eyes, even though they had known her for years. She knew then that it was fruitless. What she also knew was that she needed to be careful. She had recently read online that a woman living alone was murdered by her neighbors, allegedly because of rumors that she had invited a man up to her apartment. The thought of how they put her dead body through a virginity detection test to make sure she had been "innocent" made Nour's stomach churn.

She switched off the memory like a light switch. Now was the time to decompress. She tried to focus on beauty instead, and she was determined to find it on her walk. Unlike most people, instead of seeing the chaos of Cairo's streets as a mess, Nour saw it in a different light. Through her eyes, it was almost art. Her walking journeys often filled her with new ideas of things to paint. She allowed the sounds and noises, the people and places all fused together and graced by nature's touches, to tell her what her paintbrush should soon create. But as an artist and, therefore, an avid observer of the world, she could clearly see the darkness in it too. Everywhere. No matter how much she tried not to.

As if on command, the familiar feeling of anxiety crawled out of its hiding place and made itself at home in the corner of her brain. *Okay, refreshment. That's what I need.* Luckily, she knew a kiosk on her way to the corniche. With the crisp sound of the can opening, she leaned against the street light, scrolling and distracting herself with her story replies. A lot of them were positive remarks about her outfit or the view, but, of course, her mind singled out the negative ones.

One man replied with a sneering comment about her pixie haircut. *Classic. A fan favorite.* Nour had no idea why this haircut brought so many unwanted comments to women in Egypt, but she speculated it was either because it gave off the impression that she was "wild", "foreign", or maybe "too masculine". *That, I can take. Mild. Next!* As she scrolled away, she found the reply she was actually looking for. The one she was most afraid to see. A woman wrote: "I used to love following you when you were a *hijabi*. You lost all of my respect. Repent for your sins and rethink your life choices." Nour had lost count of the number of similar comments she had seen since posting her first photo after she removed her *hijab*. It was the most interaction she had gotten on any of her posts. It was also around that time that her anxiety took off and soared. She could not stop reading the comments that tormented her soul. People called her awful names, disrespected her, cursed her father and family. But in their eyes, all that was justified, even though the person they called those names was reading them and crying herself to sleep every night.

The soda had gotten too warm, and she felt like she needed to move right now. Standing in her place, with her thoughts, was not an option. She threw the can in the trash can and walked away. Away from where she was standing and what she was feeling. Then came the most challenging part of her walk to the Nile corniche: crossing the main street. There were no traffic lights and no instructions. Only angry drivers, and pedestrians taking a leap of faith. All she could do was take one step after the other and hope for the best. But this wasn't unfamiliar to Nour, as this had been her approach to life for as long as she could remember.

There was no action or decision she could take that would shelter her from people's judgmental comments. She had dodged them all her life, the same way she sidestepped the speeding cars now as she attempted to get to the other side. When she was a *hijabi*, she was perceived by some friends as less fun, and they were surprised every time she did something that was, in their opinion, empowering. On several occasions, she had been denied entry to certain high-end venues because she was veiled. However, sometimes they said they would compromise, but only if she wore her *hijab* in a turban style to make the guests more comfortable. Years later, when she removed her *hijab*, she was mercilessly attacked once more. She had been called an atheist, a slut, and a traitor to her religion by her social media followers, and faced less direct but equally-as-hurtful comments by acquaintances and family members. Perhaps most hurtful to Nour was how a group of childhood friends shunned her. The veil seemed to mean many things to people, except a personal choice.

And so did her divorce. When she and her ex-husband announced that they were getting a divorce, her in-laws had turned on her and blamed her for everything, even though it was a mutual decision between her and her husband at the time. They told her she must have not taken care of him, cooked for him, taken care of herself enough to be attractive to him. None of which was true, but her then-husband had watched their attack saying nothing. But even if he had, they would always have found a way to make it her fault.

To society, she had failed. So slowly, she found herself withdrawing from everyone and living in her own bubble of safety. She barely had friends and had stopped going to large family gatherings altogether. The decision to cut off extended family was not easy because it caused her parents to stop talking to her for months. But eventually she broke down and opened up to them about how she was treated by family members, especially after her divorce. She had been the pitiful relative for long enough, and she couldn›t take it anymore. Unfortunately even outside family gatherings, the judgment persevered. People eyed the divorced status on her national ID suspiciously, and new acquaintances, learning that she had chosen to part ways with her husband simply because they weren't compatible, loved to tell her how much of a wrong decision it had been to lose a good man and live without a backbone to support her. When her mother had seen the updated 'divorced status' on her ID, she had started a fight and told her that women usually lied about their social status to avoid the stigma of being a divorcee. And with that, Nour had yet another reason to add to her list of why her existence was a shame to her family.

A deafening car horn pierced her eardrums. Looking to her right, she saw a driver shouting profanities at her for apparently being in his way. He was traditional with his insults until she heard him say a moderately rare one. Ironically, she assumed his insult in many countries would have been a compliment: a lioness. In other cultures, the lioness is a symbol of undeniable strength. After all, the lioness is a powerful animal. Fierce, protective, unbeatable. Legendary. But that was not the trait Egyptians chose to focus on. It was the amount of mating encounters that the lioness supposedly had, even though for that to happen, there was also a male involved. But that didn't surprise Nour. Nothing did anymore. She cursed him back, and he drove away aggressively, almost running her over in the process.

Nour reached the other side of the road vowing not to walk all the way back again in the dark. She breathed a sigh of relief and pain. A sigh she recognized because she had heard her mother, and almost every woman she had known, do so in their life. *Yes, trying to please people is always a losing game.* And Nour knew she had lost that game a long time ago. She checked almost every single box of sin in the eyes of society. She had removed her *hijab*, she was divorced, she was living alone instead of her family's home, *and* she even had a "boyish" haircut. It would be a lie to say that their perception of her didn't affect her at all. She looked up as a plane zoomed above the city, the roar of its engines bringing an image of escape.

She knew better than that, though. She knew there was probably nowhere on Earth where being born females did not come with consequences tied to their destiny the moment they uttered their first cry. Even though lots of countries tried to pretend otherwise, the pain prevailed. Years ago, when she was doing her Fine Arts master's degree in Paris, she had seen it firsthand. The hatred in people's eyes the moment their eyes lay on her then-*hijab*, like it was an insult to their very being, even though it was a piece of cloth. And as their eyes fluttered over her, their glances screamed "terrorist". Political and social debates about the *hijab* were sparking up all over the country and were still taking place even after she graduated and left.

That experience never left her. A month after removing her *hijab*, as she sat in her bed, thoughts reeling from the comments on her *hijab*-less photo, anxiety rocking her body back and forth like a wailing sea, in an act of desperation, she resorted to writing as an outlet:

I get up in the morning, and I'm ready to conquer the world.
I tie a scarf around my head and feel myself glow with confidence.
They look at me in bewilderment: "Aren't you ashamed?"
Words like bullets are fired at me.
Oppressed, they call me. Terrorist, they scream. Ignorant, powerless, you'll never know freedom.
Take off that scarf, they command me. Don't you know what you've done?
When all I want to do is live.

I get up in the morning, and I'm ready to conquer the world.
I feel the sun on my skin and the wind rushing through my hair.
They look at me in bewilderment: "Aren't you ashamed?"
Words like daggers are thrown at me.
Slut. Whore. You'll be dragged by your hair through the fiery
pits of Hell.
Cover yourself up, they say. Don't you know what you've done?
When all I want to do is live.
But the one thing they all agree on is,
When it comes to me, my body is the only thing that matters.
It is a weapon.
It is a curse.
It is anything but mine.

There was no possible escape from being judged as a woman. She knew that then, and she knew it now. The realization was as suffocating as it was freeing. She was never going to win. No matter how much she tried. So she stopped trying.

She watched the world go by for a while, then she made her way towards the metro. She didn't feel like walking in the open any more.

Mariam
Part Two

Even though I think I'm probably dead, I know for a fact that I have never felt so alive. I am fearless. I am liberated. I am unbreakable.

Busy street, narrow street, secluded street, ancient street, gorgeous street; street after street I roam. I do not stop, I do not look back. I forget where I began, and I have no intention of figuring out where I end. The past, whatever it was, no longer weighs me down. I am so incredibly light. I have never felt so free.

I notice certain details in my surroundings for the first time. I take them all in. To me, the city of Cairo looks like a heart. A living beating heart, following a rhythm only its people could understand. Everyone around me seemed to be following this mysterious beat, to the backdrop of car horns and sunrays and magic. Leap of faith after another. Faith etched in their smiles, their strides. All of this can be seen on a busy street at rush hour if you pay enough attention, and I have all the time in the world it seems. To the foreign eye, this may seem like hopeless chaos, but it isn't. This chaos follows a beat. They just don't understand it.

So for days and nights I roam the streets. I fall in love with moments, with people, and with hidden street corners. The days are golden, the nights are silvery blue, and I am glowing. I discover quiet little bookstores whose owners are as devoted to their stores' walls as they are to their families, and I see old people with time machines for brains. These creatures are fascinating because while they seem like normal human beings, same as everyone around them, with a mere trip into the depths of their memories, they can tell you about a time in the past that you can never experience. Oh, what I wouldn't give for seeing what they so clearly do.

I linger for a day around a family living in a tiny boat floating on the Nile and come to understand the simplest pleasures of life. I laugh at jokes told by a buoyant old man entertaining an entire *qahwa* and mourn with him when he speaks of his recently deceased wife. I follow a pack of stray dogs for a day, and my admiration for them grows even deeper. I finally discover what they get up to on a daily basis and satisfy my inner wandering child. I hang around at an aging confectioner's shop for a while, observe the different customers who come by and listen to their excited conversations about the events of the day. I am fascinated by the number of occasions, life events, and celebrations that people can have in a single day. Even more amazing is how different a single occasion can be for different people. Birthdays can be a day of joy and gratitude for some; for others, a reminder of past birthdays spent feeling unloved and unwanted.

There are different things that come with being in the state I'm in. I have the ability to see something I'm sure no human has been able to witness before: only some people seem to have a slight glow about them. I notice that most children have this glistening halo. Most adults do not. I wonder if this is because when people are young, they haven't yet seen much of the world and its pain. But the older they get, the more they experience. So their souls get tired. They darken, they shrivel. They don't glow that brightly anymore.

For days, maybe months, I live the lives of many people, avoiding my own past and the questions I could not bring myself to answer. But I remember more and more as time goes by and I see glimpses of my past self in others. I shun my past; push it away. But it always tries to crawl back. One question in particular keeps floating at the back of my mind, begging to be answered. If the world is this beautiful, why did I not love it as much back then? It does not take long for the answers to finally come to me. And with them, my troubled state of mind.

Basma

*In a parallel universe, love would be left to thrive, boundless,
effortless, limitless…*

It made her heart happy seeing Farida in an engagement dress. She had been with her when she bought it, but seeing her wearing it now was something else. Her arms were starting to get sore from trying to film every second of her best friend's special day.

After the couple exchanged rings to the traditional beat of *Ya Deblet El Khotooba*, Basma decided she could now take a break from filming for a while. Farida's apartment was usually comfortable, but was now full to the brim with engagement party guests. It was difficult to find a place to relax for a second, so Basma walked over and out onto the balcony of the Heliopolis apartment.

She took a deep breath, the first in a while. The balcony was refreshingly quiet in comparison to the chaos inside. Her body relaxed, and her eyes started to adjust to the lack of artificial brightness.

Just as she was about to move closer to the railing, someone called her name from the darkness to her left, and she jumped in fright.

"Sorry, Basma, I thought you knew I was here!"

It was Farida's older brother, Karim. He attempted to stifle his laughter.

"And you're laughing too. Nice … thanks for that," she said jokingly.

"I'm sorry, I'm sorry. The way you looked … you just jumped so high. I couldn't hold it in."

Basma rolled her eyes at him. "Why are you hiding out here anyway?"

"Just taking a break from the crowd inside."

"Yes, same."

Karim walked to the balcony railing and leaned onto it. "Enjoying the party?"

"Yes, very much. Farida looks amazing." This was their first conversation that extended past "How are you? I'm fine," since he had just recently come back from living abroad for a couple of years.

An awkward silence stretched before them, so Basma cleared her throat. "What about you?"

He looked at his sister in the hall and said, "It's a bit strange seeing my little sister grow up so suddenly. It's, like, she was a kid five minutes ago, you know? But I'm happy as long as she is. Omar is a good guy."

Basma walked over and joined him at the railing. "I agree. Seems like yesterday we were graduating from college together, but she decided to abandon me and be a grown up. Such a traitor."

Karim chuckled. "Can I tell you something a bit random?"

"Umm, yes sure." she said.

"You know I want to thank you for being there for Farida these past few months."

He seemed really sincere. She shook her head. "No need to say that. She's like my sister."

"I know."

There was a long pause before Basma said, "She's grateful for you too, by the way. I saw the way you tried to cheer her up today. I'm sure she appreciates it more than you know."

His reaction was not what she was expecting. He lowered his head slightly as if in sadness. "Thanks for saying that."

She frowned. "Are you upset about something?"

He looked back up at her with an air of feigned positivity. "No, no, I'm good."

"You know you don't have to say that you're good if you're not, right?"

"Oh, I wasn't aware this balcony was a therapist's office."

She laughed. "It is now."

That seemed to cheer him up a bit, but she actually wanted to help him feel better.

"It's totally fine if you don't want to share. But I mean … it's a great opportunity. We might not even talk again."

"Good point," he joked, then remained silent again. He then said, "It's just … I think today was the bare minimum for me to do. Not nearly enough. Nothing will be enough, really."

"Why do you say so?"

"It's just that I … I feel like I wasn't there for them for the past few years when I was abroad. I thought we had more time when Baba got sick. But I was wrong. I feel like I let them all down. I think I was being selfish, you know?"

Basma took a few seconds to register this moment of rare honesty from another human being. She looked down and out at the street. A few cars zoomed by, and one of the street lights was flickering on and off. "Can I tell you something?" she said.

He nodded. "Sure."

"You are Farida's favorite person, besides me of course. But you have no idea how much she cares about you and looks up to you. You are more than a brother to her. You are a friend. And she always, always tells me how you keep the family together. So I don't think she ever felt abandoned by you."

She looked back at the party crowd.

"What is it?"

"You know Farida hates being all emotional, and she'd kill me if she knew I said any of this, so I hope this stays between us."

He looked down for a few moments, as if taking it all in. "I won't tell her. Thanks, Basma. I really needed to hear that today."

"That's what therapists do, right?"

"Right." His expression changed from amused to concerned. "Do you mind if we go inside?" he said, as he slowly moved forward and stood between her and the railing.

"Is something wrong?" she said and looked at where he was staring.

There was a middle-aged man in an undershirt on the balcony across the street smoking a cigarette and staring right at her. He saw her looking and smiled.

Her skin crawled. She looked down at her dress. "Sure, let's go inside."

For the rest of the event, Basma couldn't help but watch Karim.

He seemed very insistent on making sure everything went as smoothly as possible, and hopped in to dance with his sister whenever her smile dropped. When a song about family played, and the groom's mother and father gathered around him, Karim immediately took his mother's arm under his, guiding her towards Farida, twirling them both, and attempted to make them both laugh. Perhaps he was trying to replace the role that their late father would have filled. Basma hoped it was enough to make this moment easier for Farida because it had only been a short period since his passing. Thankfully, Farida seemed emotional but okay.

Basma made sure to stay with Farida until all the guests had left. It was now past midnight. She squeezed Farida in the tightest goodbye hug she could muster until Farida started to complain.

"How are you getting home?" Karim asked Basma.

"I'm calling Mama, and she'll pick me up."

"No way. Don't let Tante drive this late. I'm already dropping Tante Rania home, so do you mind if I drop you off too?"

Basma tried to protest because she felt like a nuisance, but when Farida's mother joined in the argument, it was to no avail. Secretly, she was glad.

When Karim parked in front of Basma's building, Basma was practically daydreaming about finally falling asleep. Tante Rania's house was farther away than she thought.

"Thank you so much for driving me back. I really appreciate it."

"It's truly nothing."

"You were already home—"

"Don't worry, I actually love to drive,"

When she looked at him suspiciously, he protested with a laugh. "I swear!"

"Fine."

"Can you send me the pictures before you go?" he asked

"Of course."

The four hundred pictures and videos started to travel from her phone to his.

A police car's loud honk split the silence of the night.

A policeman stepped out of the car and walked over to them.

Karim rolled down his window.

"What are you two doing?"

"Sitting in the car. What's the issue?"

"Just making sure." He gave Basma a stare she didn't feel comfortable with. She tugged down at her dress. The last time she was dressed nicely for an event, she was driving her own car, alone, and at a checkpoint, the policeman insisted she get out and hand him her driver's license himself. Just so he could have a good look at her body. She was grateful that day that nothing more happened.

"What was that!" Karim said when the policeman left.

"You've been in Canada for a while, haven't you? He … was making sure we weren't, you know."

"No way! What's it to him!" he said, visibly getting worked up.

"Hey, nothing you can do about it. That's the way things are. Let's not look for more trouble."

Despite the ending, it was a good day.

Over time, they saw much more of each other.

They started to go out with Farida and her now-fiancé, then with Farida and Basma's friends.

To Basma, he was just another person to keep at a distance, just another friend with whom to fill the long hours of her life with some laughter and jokes. After past friendships she thought would last forever had ended in ways she never would have foreseen, and past relationships ending in ways that were even worse, she had decided that being by herself was the safest place to be.

She liked it that way. People to her were just static to fill the emptiness. But he did not seem to get that. He would seek her out amidst the white noise of chatter in an outing and start a conversation, ask her questions that made her uncomfortable, not because they were in any way rude, but because they repeatedly caught her off guard. They were not the type of questions she was used to. They threatened to pull her out of her skin, survey her, reveal her, make her vulnerable.

On one of the group's many sushi outings, he did it again.

When everyone was busy talking, he turned to her. "Are you actually this happy, or do you just fake this smile all the time?"

"What do you even mean? Why do you keep asking me these questions!"

"How many worlds do you think there are?"

"You're officially crazy," she said laughingly, looking around at the rest of her friends engaged in casual conversations. She was torn between a desire to join them and a feeling of curiosity as to where this path might lead her.

"Well, the normal answer is one," he said, ignoring her. "But just think about it for a second. Just listen. We don't all have identical life experiences, right?"

"Right."

"So it's only logical that we don't see the world exactly the same way. I like to talk to people, listen to them, and see the world through their eyes."

"Well go explore someone else's world," she said. She never knew what would come out of this guy's mouth next.

"But yours is fascinating to me."

Their conversations usually went on and on and on, trailing off into deeper and more bizarre topics until she started to wonder whether maybe, just maybe, this should be the norm, and the people who talked about the traffic or the weather were the ones who were insane. She got more comfortable with time, comfortable with his random questions that he uttered as naturally as asking for directions to a doctor's office. And slowly but surely, he went from being her best friend's brother to another best friend.

11 March - 3 pm

Basma: How was the interview?

Karim: Not sure. Don't think I did well to be honest.

Basma: What is it with you and not feeling good enough?

Karim: Yeah, you're right.

Basma: Say it with me. I am Karim, and I am amazing!

Karim: Hmm … so you think I'm amazing?

Basma: No.

5 April - 11 pm

Basma: Your post just came up on my feed. Thanks for posting about that rape case. Thanks for all your women empowerment posts actually. I rarely see any men talking about it.

Karim: Really? I'm not sure that's true.

Basma: Do you know how many men are talking about this case on my timeline right now? You and you. Go look at your timeline right now.

Karim: Okay, so I checked. I hate it when you're right. Why do you think that is, though?

Basma: Because it doesn't affect them.

Karim: I don't know ... I don't think it has anything to do with whether or not something affects you.

Basma: I don't know. A guy friend told me they feel like nothing will change if they do speak.

Karim: Maybe it doesn't change because they don't.

21 April - 2 am

Karim: I'm telling you, I can always tell whether a person is an older or younger sibling. I could almost immediately tell from Farida's stories about you that you were the oldest.

Basma: Yes … sure you did.

Karim: Well, it's true. Even if you choose not to believe in my powers.

Basma: Okay, enlighten me then. How could you tell?

Karim: Well, I'm the oldest, so there were so many similarities.

Basma: Such as?

Karim: Well, you immediately try to fix a situation. Remember when we were talking on the balcony? You immediately gave me a therapy session.

Basma: Okay, valid.

Karim: There's more. You're the person to take immediate responsibility in any situation. Farida didn't even arrange the engagement; you did.

Basma: Fair enough, any more analyses of my personality?

16 May - 2 am

Karim: What did you enjoy most on your trip to Dahab?

Basma: The day before.

Karim: Basma … go to sleep.

Basma: I'm being serious.

Karim: Okay, I'll go with it. Why?

Basma: This is going to sound strange.

Karim: I like strange.

Basma: I always like events more before they happen. I like the way they look in my head. I like the waiting and the anticipation more than the thing itself. I like things while they glisten and shine away from me, because when I get there, they always disappoint me. My expectations ruin things most of the time. Not sure if I'm making any sense.

Karim: I don't think that's strange. We just need to make the events in your life better than your expectations, that's all.

Basma: I admire your confidence, but that's impossible.

Karim: Try me.

———·◆◆◆·———

As the weeks passed by, she gradually felt differently about him. Maybe the heat of the rapidly approaching summer was starting to get to her head, but she doubted it was that.

One day during an online meeting, she found herself scrawling away in the corner of her notes, doodling nonsense, the voice of the attendees a distant hum. He kept popping in her head whenever she thought about anything, something he did, something he said. Or simply his presence. She was thrown off balance. He wouldn't go away or leave her head alone, and she couldn't understand why.

She was thinking of how he could always make her feel better, and the way he always knew what she was thinking. She loved how he always made fun of himself and the way he teased her until she got so annoyed that she had to yell at him. She loved how he could make friends anywhere and the way he always stood up for what he believed in, not caring in the slightest about what anyone else thought of him. And above all, she loved how he made her a better person by pushing her to do things she wouldn't otherwise do.

Her thoughts came to a halt, her eyes widening involuntarily, and she cursed inside her head. *Am I starting to have feelings for him?*

Nothing scared her more than that. She was always around other people. Had too many friends. But always made sure she kept them all at a distance, except perhaps Farida, but even that had taken years. She knew that allowing someone to get close to her core, close enough to touch it, meant that they were close enough to cause her pain.

That was when she started to hold back. Both intentionally and unintentionally. She wouldn't text him for weeks at a time, and when he texted her, she was much colder than before. The friendship eventually fizzled out.

On their next outing as a group, when she saw him, she knew she had been right. The feelings didn't go away. His outer shell made her stare, but it was what was inside him that made her melt; he makes her laugh, and she evaporates. He says her name, and she turns into nothingness.

But he wasn't alone.

Another girl was clinging to his arm, and they were laughing together. All through the outing, they joked and laughed. Every time Basma looked at them, it hurt even more. She was normally a calm, controlled person, but on that day, it was so much harder to breathe.

A few days later, he wouldn't stop texting her. Then he started to call. Eventually, she gave in and picked up the phone.

"Why haven't you been answering any of my texts? I was worried about you."

"Sorry, I was just busy with work."

"It's Friday, Basma."

"Can we talk later? I have a deadline," she lied.

"I'll be under your building in twenty minutes. Get dressed."

"I said I was busy, Karim."

"Get dressed."

When they hung up, she threw her phone onto the bed. *Why is he always so pushy?* Then, panic set in. Even though she knew nothing was going to happen between them, she didn't want to look awful, and right now she did. At the same time, she didn't want to make him feel like she had made an effort. Eventually, she decided to just put up her hair in a ponytail and throw on a white t-shirt. *Totally natural.*

In the car, Basma stared out the window, trying not to look at him. Her heart was pounding, she was amazed how he couldn't hear it.

"So are you going to just keep facing away like that?"

"Sorry. Just not in a great mood, that's all."

"Fine. Let's do something fun then. You always said you wanted to try *hommos el sham* by the Nile before, right? Let's do that."

She tried to make up excuses, but he said it would be a really quick trip. She didn't know what else to say.

All through the ride, she felt his eyes on her. She tried to be normal or at least fake it, but couldn't. She had never in her life failed this badly at anything.

They parked near the corniche. Lots of people were out for a stroll on the weekend.

When he got back into the car with the *hommos el sham*, she reached for her cup. But he dodged her hand and put both in the cupholder.

"What?" she asked, annoyed.

"What was wrong with you the last time we went out?" He looked right into her eyes.

"When was that?" she said, looking away.

"When we were in Maadi."

"I was just not feeling well. I actually said that if you had bothered to listen." She remembered the girl again and felt the cruel, cool blade of jealousy slash through her skin.

"You're lying."

That was an answer she was not expecting. She had predicted that this was going to be a casual conversation and then they would part ways and forget about it. He looked her straight in the eyes again.

"You're lying, Basma, and you don't like to lie."

For an instant, she panicked, not knowing what to say next.

"You know, I didn't understand why you had pushed me away for such a long time until we could barely talk anymore. It hurt me more than you know. I asked myself a million times what I could have done wrong. I didn't understand until I saw the way you looked at me and Lina that day."

She felt her face flame with embarrassment: had she been that obvious?

"For a person who always claims to be so smart, you're not as clever as you think you are. I've had feelings for you for a very long time, but I thought that you didn't care much about me, especially when you completely shut me out. I took that as a message and forced myself to move on. I respected your feelings. But I still do, and probably always will, so there!" he said angrily. "Stop running away from your emotions like they're dangerous. It's okay to be human. It's okay to be weak. It's okay for you to let people in every once in a while. It won't kill you. You're missing out on everything worth anything in this world. What's wrong with you?! Honestly, you drive me mad!"

When he stopped talking, she stared at the rise and fall of his chest, not knowing how to react. Eventually, she looked at his face, still contorted with rage, and then, for some reason, she laughed. A laugh that seemed like it had been imprisoned inside her for a very long time, finally free, finally escaping. Immediately after, he laughed too.

"So do you have anything to say to that, or should I just throw your cup away right now?"

"No."

"Okay, at least look me in the eyes then."

She tried, but couldn't.

"Still nothing, huh?"

"Yes, I do have something to say."

"Am I going to hear it soon, or?"

She looked back at him. "I … feel the same way."

He looked away and then back at her, his smile almost too wide to contain.

"You look so shy, it's adorable."

"Oh, my God. Stop!" she said, shoving him as hard as she could.

He didn't even flinch. "You should know that I really do like you a lot, Basma. I see this going somewhere long term. You make me really, really happy. I haven't felt this way before, and I don't go around saying this to anyone. It was a bit strange at first seeing as you're my sister's best friend. But to me, it's no longer strange anymore. Not in the slightest."

"It feels normal to me too. I don't know why I can't be normal right now. You're making me nervous and I really, truly, with every fiber of my being hate that."

He stared at her for quite some time until she eventually told him, "Are you going to say anything?"

He nodded. "Is it okay if I give you a hug?"

"Yes," she said breathlessly.

She couldn't remember ever feeling happier than she did at that moment, hugging someone who had managed to make her feel safer than she ever did. More accepted than she ever did. Happier than she ever did.

Although it had only been seconds, it felt much, much longer. It felt like relief.

She then heard aggressive knocks on the car window. "What do you think you're doing?" a random man shouted.

"That's none of your business. Who are you to ask me?" shouted Karim.

"You don't go hugging women in the street like that."

"What's it to you?!"

"Have some morals, you prick. Take your prostitute to a private place. Or at least share."

Karim got out of the car. "How dare you!"

It all then happened too fast for Basma to understand. A physical fight broke out. Karim jumped onto the man, punching him in the face. Then everything was a blur, she couldn't tell who was hitting whom. Men and women gathered around. The man's face was covered in blood.

When onlookers separated the two, the man insisted on taking Karim to the police station.

They stayed at the station for hours. Farida kept telling Basma to leave. That Basma's being there did nothing to help the situation.

When her mother called her, asking where she was, she had to leave. She didn't feel like telling her what had happened or where she was. She didn't feel like talking to anyone for that matter.

She saw the metro across the street. Her phone was about to die. Without thinking, she walked towards it. She just needed to be home right now.

What was supposed to be one of the best moments of her life was ruined. The memory tainted forever by people she didn't even know. A stranger who called her names and hit a man who had committed no crime.

Looking back, she realized this wasn't the only beautiful moment that a stranger had ruined for them for the mere fact that she was alone with a man. If there weren't comments, there were stares. Stares that told her exactly what they thought of her. Even though all she wanted was to be safe with the man she had come to love.

She could not count the number of times she was cat-called on the street and not a single soul batted an eye, but if it was love, if it was touch with her consent, touch that she actually wanted, that was forbidden.

It was then that she realized the judgment had always been there. Eyes on them. All the time. Everywhere.

Farida called her to tell her that things were getting resolved, but still, as she approached the metro station that day, all she could think about was how many more of their moments those eyes would ruin.

Fatma

In a parallel universe, her body would merely be her physical existence, and not an excuse for her demise.

A series of lush, green mountains materialized before her. She was sitting on top of the highest mountain, looking down at the world. The world which she had come to fear so much had been transformed into the contents of a child's toy chest. Trains, buses, people, buildings. Everything felt so insignificant. All the worries poisoning her brain had softly melted away. She looked down at this miniature land and it did not scare her in the slightest. All she wanted was to just lie there, just a quiet moment to herself, free of worry, free of fear in a world that was her own and in which she felt safe, and in which her every movement was not tracked by hungry eyes. All her desires were met in the dream. It was like a refuge, an escape.

Looking out onto the world from the mountain top, she saw the sun setting, painting the world with golden light. Then, there was chaos.

The buildings kept getting larger until they dwarfed her frame and suffocated her. Then, dozens of buses sped by, almost running her over in the process. She ran, but she wasn't fast enough. Shadowy people appeared and walked towards her. Men had their arms outstretched as they approached her. They were laughing. She was trying to move in the opposite direction, when a car horn from right behind her made her stop in her tracks.

Fatma opened her eyes and almost cried.

She could actually hear the car horn even though the windows were shut. Following that were the sounds of men and women fighting. Apparently, there was a fight. Nothing out of the ordinary in her neighborhood.

She hated being awake. This was the first sentiment she felt. As her brain registered it, she stared blankly at her surroundings and started to enter her daily state of numbness. After fifteen minutes of trying to force her day to a start, Fatma put on her school uniform consisting of a loose white shirt with long sleeves, a tie, and a long black skirt which reached her toes, now clad in black worn-out flats. She tied her only yellowing white head scarf and walked out of the room that she shared with two younger sisters. She didn't bother to look in the mirror. And why should she? Whether she was pretty or not did not seem to matter. Men would stare at her anyway. She was even told by a girlfriend once that some men have a fetish for full-on black *abayas*. There was nothing she could do to her appearance that would work to keep them away, except maybe an invisibility cloak.

On her way out, the familiar scent of hashish brushed against her nostrils, and she heard the daily taunts from her unemployed and bitter father's mouth. He loved to tell her every single day that he hated wasting his money on a girl's education, even though he didn't spend one pound on her. He had hit her last night, when he was too high or too drunk or maybe both. She didn't understand why he hit her, but she had stopped trying to find reasons a long time ago. She just accepted it as her reality. She could feel the bruise on her arm brush against her uniform. It didn't hurt that bad. There had been much worse ones.

Pushing the chipped wooden door, which was four steps away from every part of the house, she was finally outside. She rarely felt anything at all, but feelings of pity for her mother always made an unwelcome appearance at this very time of day. Images of her mother's withered hands and wrinkled face filled her head. Her mother had that kind of presence that anyone could completely miss out on if they weren't paying much attention as she dutifully catered to the needs of the family without being truly there. She wished her mother would get a divorce from her father, but she knew she kept him in her life even though she made all the income so people would not have anything to say about her honor and her family.

Fatma descended the stairs, not bothering to pay attention to her steps. There were chips at the edge of stair number four, fourteen, sixteen and twenty seven, which she avoided like an expert. All the while, she could hear voices emerging from every other apartment in the dust-covered, dimly-lit atmosphere. Other than that, nothing gave life to the otherwise dead silent staircase.

Down the dusty stairs and into the unbearable heat, she started her daily routine of survival and self-loathing. Through her walk to the all-girls school many blocks away, she escaped into a world of her own because living in reality would only mean that she would see the condition of the street, sniff the unexplainable odors, and hear the rude comments flying at her occasionally. Men, young and old, and even boys, had a way of making her squirm with the urge to sink into the gravel road and disappear forever. She could see them from the corner of her eyes, their eyes on her body, tracing it as she walked. She could almost feel their gaze touching her skin. On she walked.

In the past, she didn't see the world that way. As a little girl, she saw the street as a playground that she could run to when bored. But around the time she turned twelve, this changed. Her mother had given her a speech she had never forgotten.

"You're grown up now, and some things need to change. The clothes you used to wear will no longer be appropriate. You need to wear looser clothes. As for your behavior," she had said, "I expect you to start acting more like a respectable lady, no more running around the streets like a child, and speak as little as you can with boys. We don't need the neighbors talking about us, do we? An honorable young woman does not draw attention to herself, so I expect much more mature behavior from you from now on, do you understand?"

At the time, her mother's words hung in the air between them, and she knew the carefree days of childhood, of running around in the street playing games with the neighbors, were over. Even though she couldn't put it into words back then, she later learned that her body was changing, to society every curve was a crime, so she needed to be careful.

Fatma tugged at her shirt to make it looser than it was and adjusted her scarf to cover more of her forehead, trying to cover as much of the crime scene as she could. She did her best to be as invisible as possible. She stared at her feet and forced herself to be hypnotized by their rhythm and pretended she didn't exist.

Suddenly, in the back of her mind, she could hear his awful words. A man was verbally harassing her. In the back of her mind, his words were scornful and said with such malice that she doubted that he could be human. As reality started to come into perspective, she realized that it wasn't in her mind anymore. It was really happening. Her steps became just a little louder and just a little faster. She said to herself that if she could just get away, all of it would disappear. But this made it worse.

She heard him come off his Vespa, laughing and calling her sarcastically—and then it happened. He groped her. She paused, her body unresponsive, full to the brim with panic, anger, and humiliation.

He was laughing again, and she felt distant somehow from the situation, as if it was happening to someone else. Trembling, she turned to face him and screamed and cursed at him at the top of her voice. His expression turned from scornful to angry. He grabbed her by her head scarf and a chunk of hair underneath and pulled her as if she had been the one who wronged him.

In the midst of all the panic, she hadn't realized that they were the spectacle of the entire street. Men and women formed a circle around them, two of whom held the harasser back and ordered her to get back. Still distant from her body, she cursed and cursed, screaming until her throat was on fire.

This is when a middle-aged woman spoke to her with a disapproving tone. "Stop making such a scene, will you? Aren't you ashamed? Maybe next time you should dress better and try not to draw so much attention to yourself."

Even those who had sympathized with Fatma came to the harasser's defense when she continued screaming.

"It's okay, Miss. Let it go. Don't make a fuss out of it. Why ruin his life by screaming for the police? He's already leaving."

After that, she had walked away with all the dignity she could muster until she crossed to the other side of the street. She tried to adjust her headscarf with shaking hands, but before she knew it, she was sobbing and half sat, half collapsed onto the sidewalk.

Fatma could still feel the eyes of the people on her, so she stumbled as she stood up and walked away as fast as she could back home. She couldn't think at this point. It was as if her body had taken control, so on she walked. Her brain started registering what had happened, trying to make sense of the scene. The harasser's scornful expression. Then the pure hatred in his eyes. The feeling of his hands on her. The way her head was throbbing where he pulled her hair. The pungent smell of his sweat. The way people looked at her when she wouldn't let it go.

As if time itself was warped, she found herself approaching her building quicker than she could comprehend. And under the building, she saw her mother. She blinked again and again, trying to make sure she was really there. When she didn't disappear, relief flooded Fatma's body, and she almost ran into her mother's arms.

"Fatma, what is it! Are you hurt?"

When Fatma started to cry, her mother added, "Let's go behind the building. You're making a scene."

With fearful eyes, and a firm grip on her daughter's arm, she pushed her forward and away from prying eyes.

"What is it?" said her mother in a hushed tone.

"A guy … a guy on the street." She stuttered through her tears. "A guy on the street touched me … on my way to school. And I tried to fight, but … but people defended him … and I didn't know what to do."

"You shouted in the middle of the street?"

"Of course I did. I was trying to make him stop."

"So you let the whole area know you were touched by some man?"

"What was I supposed to do?"

"In my time, when someone bothered us on the street, we used to not give them attention."

"And look where that brought us. Your daughter is still getting harassed on the street exactly the way you were. Nothing changed, because you didn't do anything about it!"

"Watch your tongue when talking to me."

"I'm sorry, okay? But you're not helping me. I don't know what to do. I … I can't make myself stop crying."

"Calm down and toughen up. These things happen every day. And haven't I told you before not to wear that skirt? It's getting too tight. And that strand of hair you're so proud to display should not show. I tried to warn you."

Through sobs, Fatma listened, uncomprehending at first, to what she had thought would be a comforting and understanding speech like medicine for her inner wounds. But her mother's words turned out to be worse than the attack itself. They were acid. After that, the tears stopped, and she didn't feel anything but numbness, the state in which she had always existed.

"Now straighten yourself up before you go up and your father sees this. Or, worse, your brother. He shouldn't find out, or he won't be as easy on you as I am. He might even find the man and beat him up. He could go to jail for it."

"I need to go," Fatma said, turning around and walking away.

"Excuse me, who do you think you are? I didn't say you could go."

Her mother attempted to hold her back.

"Don't touch me, let go!"

Her mother continued saying things, but as the distance grew between them, Fatma knew her mother was not going to raise her voice in public. And she was right.

So she walked.

She walked until her feet ached, and light turned to dark, and she was very far away from home. And until she couldn't move any further.

She sent her friend Heba a message saying she was coming over.

But Heba's house was nowhere near, and she couldn't walk anymore. There was always the microbus, but she couldn't handle that today. Being stuck sitting next to, in front of, or behind a potentially handsy male stranger in such a confined space, with no escape. The threat could come from any direction. And she was very, very tired. Of it all.

Gamila

In a parallel universe, her youthful soul and her innocence, would last as long as she wanted it to.

Scarcely any thoughts occupied this eleven-year-old's head. She had not been taught otherwise and, therefore, did not dwell much on anything but the prospect of the day being over. Hopefully a quick journey home, and, of course, the unlikely promise of enough food.

And so, today was just like any other day. It was made up of never-ending, almost-rhythmic utterance of the same sentences as she walked unceasingly between cars at one of Maadi's most crowded traffic stops. But that didn't bother Gamila at all. Ever since she was a child, her mother had given her a clear instruction list detailing what exactly to do, so at this point, it came naturally. Her mother's list was pretty straightforward: the more cars you reach when the traffic lights turn red, the higher your chance of being given change. Don't leave as soon as drivers look away; they may change their minds, and run away if a man tries to put his hand on you. And, finally, if anyone gets aggressive, leave immediately or scream.

Gamila looked into a window of a woman wearing unusually large sunglasses. The woman closed her window and looked away in disgust. Luckily, Gamila had grown desensitized to all sorts of reactions, of which she had received millions of versions. Almost none would offend her, however harsh or rude. Even though she was never told this directly, she had realized from a young age that dignity was an unapologetic traitor as soon as hunger arrived.

The reactions she observed from the impatient drivers at the traffic stop were of a wide spectrum. Some rolled down their windows and handed her a few pounds; others even ventured as much as to smile or say a kind word, but the majority pretended not to notice her existence at all, and sometimes she wondered if she was really there and would look down at her hands to make sure.

On a few occasions, however, there had been worse reactions. She found out early on that even when she meant no harm, people could be rude with their words and even their facial reactions. When she used to cry, her mother explained that some people were under the impression that all beggars were part of organized groups with calculated schemes to gain an easy living and were carefully scattered across popular streets. With time, Gamila had found this to be true in some cases. On several occasions, as she and her mother sat cross-legged on a pavement with their usual display of tissue boxes to sell, they had been chased away by leaders of such groups and told to try elsewhere, and so they would be forced to look for another street or spot. After all, who would help them? It was Gamila and her mother against the world.

She knew her father had abandoned the family sometime after she was born for a reason she was never told, leaving her mother with four kids to raise on her own and of whom she was the youngest. The whole family lived in a makeshift home in a cemetery, entirely different from the relatively busy and vibrant streets of Maadi. But she had learned not to fear the dead. The living were much crueler than the dead could ever be.

When in the world of the living, as she was at the moment, lists and instructions, she believed, kept her safe. Anything guaranteed in this life was welcomed by Gamila. Even her daily routine was a list. Her mother woke her and her brothers up every day at 5 am. This was easy, since their home consisted of only one room, and they all slept side by side on a blanket on the floor. They then took turns washing with the hose outside and using the bathroom shared by all the other makeshift houses in the cemetery. After that, her brothers walked to school, and she and her mother took the metro to the street on which they currently begged. From then on, if she stayed within the list and the routine, all was well. She just walked from car to car and asked for change. When people looked away, she tried once more before moving on. And that was what she did for hours every day.

But, sometimes, Gamila got distracted from the list. And when she did pay attention to anything outside of it, feelings she would rather not experience often arose to the forefront of her brain, screaming to be noticed.

Seeing other children always caught her attention. Moving on from the lady with the big sunglasses, she walked over to a silver car. She peeked into the passenger window and locked eyes with a girl sitting next to an older man who, judging by the similarities in their features, Gamila deemed to be the girl's father. The girl was probably Gamila's age, or a little younger. She was holding two dolls, one brunette, the other blonde, and she seemed happy and comfortable. But most noticeable to Gamila was how the girl seemed secure inside the car, a barrier between her and the outside world, with not just one day but an entire future secured before her. Gamila didn't think the girl needed a list to feel safe. The girl extended a hand holding one of her dolls as if to offer it to her. Gamila smiled wide. But that was when the man noticed what the girl was doing and told her to look away. Before the girl could react, the traffic light turned green, and the car moved forward. Yes, seeing other children always distracted Gamila from her list and her routine. Now all she could feel was a sinking feeling at the bottom of her stomach.

She walked away from the traffic lights and onto the nearby sidewalk where her mother sat cross-legged on the pavement with her usual display of tissue boxes to try and sell.

"You seem upset. Did something happen?" asked her mother.

"No, I'm fine," she said, attempting to keep a neutral expression, but it faltered and tears glistened in her eyes.

"What is it, Gamila? Don't scare me like this."

"Nothing, I was just thinking that I want a doll."

Her mother sighed deeply and looked down, her expression something between sadness and anger.

"I'm sorry, Mama. Forget it."

"You know that if I could, I would get you whatever you ask for. But I think you can see how we are living. You don't have to make me feel worse about what I can't get you."

"I know, Mama. Please forget I said anything."

"This heat is unbearable. I can't stand it. Please look for a nearby water dispenser, and fill up this water bottle."

Gamila swallowed the lump in her throat, not only because she was straying away from her routine, but because she knew she had to walk past the bridge.

Gamila stood up and walked towards it. Her heart thumped. She was unable to peel her eyes away from a seemingly harmless spot under its shade. To everyone else, the spot under the bridge probably meant nothing. But to Gamila, it was a place that hid memories she would rather forget.

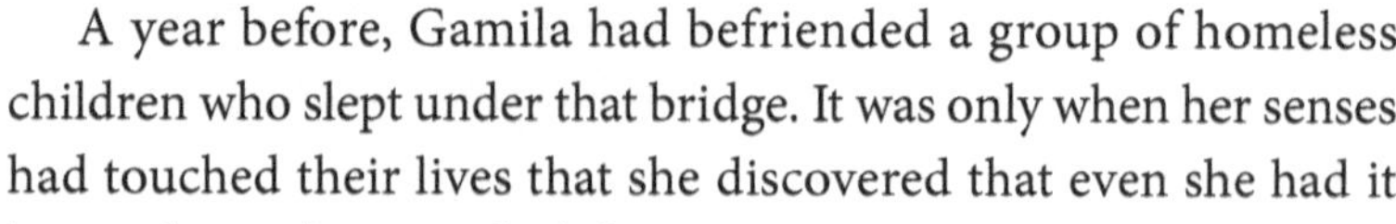

A year before, Gamila had befriended a group of homeless children who slept under that bridge. It was only when her senses had touched their lives that she discovered that even she had it better than other people did.

The group was composed of three children of different ages. One boy and two girls. In those days, Gamila used to spend most of her day around them, just passing the time, enjoying being around people her age. But with time, one by one disappeared as if being crossed off of a list. That is, if you could count them as having actually existed. When almost no one but her had truly acknowledged their existence at all.

Many things were bizarre about this trio. But perhaps the strangest, to Gamila, was why the youngest girl in the group, who was still older than Gamila, always chose to dress up as a boy.

One day, Gamila had mustered enough courage to ask.

"Reda … why do you dress and act like a boy? Do you not like being a girl?"

Reda laughed loudly. It echoed under the bridge. Then, through the occasional puffs of a cigarette, she said, "Oh, no, I liked being a girl. But this is easier."

"But … why?"

"I can get delivery jobs at local supermarkets when I can and make some cash."

"Why can't you do that as a girl?"

"They won't let me, and it's not safe," she said, stomping her cigarette out with her bare foot.

"Why is it safe as a boy and not as a girl?"

"If you don't know the answer, then you haven't seen enough of the world. You're too young to understand, so I won't blow the smoke cloud off of your innocent eyes. I won't be the one to do it. People like you are so rare in this world." Gamila didn't know if her tone had been sincere or sarcastic. Maybe both.

"But I really want to understand. I'm not a child."

"Look, not always. Some people harm boys on the street too. It's just a little less common. Nothing is guaranteed. But I'd take any chance I could get." Then she laughed again. Gamila didn't understand why.

When Gamila pleaded to know more, she was simply ignored. That was how she was treated for the most part. Even if they were just a few years older than her, they acted like they were old enough to be her parents, old enough to know better. When she grumpily told Reda this, she was told that even a year on the street was worth a decade of life experience.

Just as soon as Gamila had decided to give up on the topic altogether, Nawal, the oldest girl, approached them. She had an even more difficult story for Gamila to fully comprehend. She used to see her flirting with men in fancy-looking cars which Gamila knew was frowned upon. Girls weren't supposed to chat with men, let alone flirt with them. But Gamila knew better than to question Nawal. She scared her the most out of the three. That was why seeing Nawal walking towards her now, a menacing look filling her eyes, made her hands go numb. When Nawal reached Reda and Gamila, she looked down at Gamila like she was scum. Reda put her hand on Nawal's shoulder as if to tell her: don't. For a long moment, the two older girls looked at each other as if having a silent conversation with just their eyes. Then Reda lifted her hand off of Nawal's shoulder and walked away. Nawal, tall and thin with a body that had only just begun to blossom into womanhood, and dressed in a form-hugging black *abaya*, leaned down to Gamila's height so that they were almost eye to eye.

"Have you ever been touched by someone when you were five years old because you were a girl who grew up in an orphanage with no one to protect her? Touched against your will everywhere on your body, by someone who was supposed to care for you, no matter how much you cried?" she said, with a tone that frightened Gamila. "Have you lost your ability to feel anything because of how frequently it happened? Have you ever been forced to do the thing that you spent your entire childhood running away from because your wailing stomach just wouldn't shut up and kept you up for days at a time?" She paused for a second and stared deeper into Gamila's eyes. "I can see from the remnants of light in your eyes that you haven't. Do you know how much I would give to be you?"

Gamila stared into Nawal's eyes, paralyzed with something that was more than fear. She looked into those eyes that would have been beautiful if they hadn't been so empty, so very dead, any form of life or laughter having left them a long time ago.

"Nawal … if you were being harmed … why didn't you tell anyone?"

Nawal chuckled with a laugh that sounded worse than crying.

"Tell who, *habibty*?"

"The police. Anyone."

"You're even more naive than I thought, *habibty*. They don't care. No one does. These people, they don't see us. They don't acknowledge we exist. They don't care if we live or die. When they spot us on the street, they look away and go back to their cozy homes and their families and watch television. Then every Ramadan, they give us a little more change and drive away, thinking they are the best people on the planet. They would do anything to make their conscience feel better. Look away. Say to themselves that we chose this life or that we beg for money to buy drugs. No one cares, *habibty*. This country that calls itself religious treats us like we and the stray dogs on the street are the same."

"Nawal, that's enough."

Suddenly, Gamila was aware that Reda was back and had her hand on Nawal's shoulder. Nawal shrugged it off angrily and walked away.

"I'll handle her," said Reda. "Maybe you should sit with your mother for the rest of the day, ok?"

A loud car horn sliced the moment, causing her to jolt and look in its direction. When Gamila turned back, Reda had already walked away.

When she told her mother about what she was told, her words were met with ominous silence. Her mother, who rarely showed any emotion, looked uncomfortable.

"Children who are unprotected on the streets are sometimes taken advantage of. But don't worry. I won't let that happen to you. Ever."

A few months after that day, everything was fine, at least as fine as it could be. They sometimes begged together and they shared their *ful* sandwiches with her and so she figured she had become a member of the group. With time, she began to know more details about how each one of them had ended up on the street. Even though they looked different, and had different back stories, they were all clothed with the street. They were a few shades darker than anyone else from the dirt, pollution, and exhaustion, which had the power to make them blend into the background like camouflage, maybe just to fool the street into not devouring them whole. The bond between them was as unbreakable as it was weak, because they had never really stood a chance against the world. And gradually, it was all gone as if it had never happened.

The boy was arrested while trying to pickpocket someone. Reda, according to Nawal's words, was found and dragged away maybe to death or worse by her uncle, and Nawal herself left with a man one day and just never came back. Gamila never found out what happened to her. It all left her staring blankly at their spot under the bridge, contemplating how she may have been the only person to have known that they had ever lived there. That they had even existed.

"Get out of the way, child," a man said.

Gamila was pushed out of her memories and back into reality. She moved hurriedly out of his way.

There she was once more. Looking at the bridge. But it didn't look the same as it did before. Beneath it was a kiosk busy with customers, and to the edge of the pavement, men and women were taking shelter in the shade.

Gamila forcibly peeled her eyes away from the bridge and walked across to a narrow side street in search of the water dispenser she knew she had spotted once before. Twenty minutes of fruitless searching finally ended in success; she filled the water bottle and hurried back to her mother, careful not to look at the bridge on her way back.

"Here you go, Mama."

"You've been gone for ages; I was starting to get worried!" She snatched the water bottle from Gamila. "What took you so long?"

"I'm sorry. I forgot where it was exactly."

Her mother took a sip and simmered down. "Have a sip. It's hot."

Gamila reached out for the bottle, but her mother interrupted. "Wait. Do you see the man standing on the pavement across the street? He looks well-dressed—go after him."

Gamila complied immediately. Missing one opportunity might mean no food for the day.

She sped across the street and was cursed at by several cars, but she made it.

"Sir, would you like some tissues?" she implored with her well-practiced face.

The man turned around quickly and upon seeing her, produced a smile so warm and gentle that it caught her off guard. People would sometimes, though rarely, smile at her, but it was the sort that was more out of obligation than of being genuine. His, however, was a different kind. It was welcoming and encouraging and seemed to emerge from a genuine place. She smiled back carefully, feeling a little suspicious. Roaming the streets for so long had taught her to be wary of people's actions, even those that appeared positive, and she never let her guard down.

"What's your name?" he said

She looked across the street at her mother. "Gamila."

"Oh, really! That's my little sister's name," he said. "You remind me so much of her, but I think she's a little bit older."

He brought out his wallet from his back pocket, but before opening it, he completely surprised her by striking up a conversation.

He asked a few general questions about her day and even talked a little about his own. Through it all she obliged, but she could not for the life of her come up with a reason why he would talk so much to her. He looked her in the eyes, as if she was his equal. As if she was a person.

A minute of mostly one-sided conversation passed, and if she wasn't so curious about him, she would have been bored.

"So tell me, Gamila, do you go to school?"

"No."

"Why is that?" he said, and she noticed that his cheerful tone wavered just for a second.

"My mother took me out because she says I won't need it. My brothers still go sometimes if they're not working, but she says I will probably have a husband to work and look after me," she replied matter-of-factly.

The stranger seemed to receive this information with some evident sadness. He seemed to talk in a more serious tone now, less lighthearted than before. "Well I don't know about that." He then took a step back to stand next to her and pointed at the light-blue summer sky. "What do you think about it?"

She was momentarily taken aback by the question, but then said, "About what exactly?"

"The sky."

"Pretty."

"I agree. It *is* pretty. Very pretty. Hmm, but why do you think the sky is blue and not red like that car over there?"

"Uh, I don't really know why," she said, perplexed.

"Okay, then what about the sun? What do you think it is?"

"I don't know," she said, furrowing her eyebrows. She had not really given much thought to these things, but now the question was there in her head, and she was intrigued. "So what are the answers to your questions?"

"The sun is a star, just like the ones you can see illuminating the sky at night, but it's much closer to us. That is why it is bigger and brighter than the others." With that answer, he rummaged through his wallet and took out a staggering 200-pound note.

"Thank you so much. God bless you, sir," she said, overjoyed. Then, after a long pause, she added. "Why *is* the sky blue?"

"Go back to school, and you will find out this and so much more. I will be back to check up on you every once in a while. Make sure you're even smarter than me next time!"

He gave her his brilliant smile one last time and bid her farewell. He walked away casually and soon blended in with the growing rush hour crowd. To her, however, he was singled out from all people. It was one of the rare moments in her young life when she did not feel as invisible as the air she breathed. He saw her and talked to her as an equal, and his words echoed loudly in her head. She felt, for the first time in a long time, that maybe there was more to life than she had known.

When it was time to go home, the next step on Gamila's list was taking the metro. But the walk this time was different. Her mother was ecstatic at the amount the man had given her and promised to buy Gamila a doll.

That day was a good day.

Safaa

In a parallel universe, love would be a possible reality and not a fool's desperate hallucination.

Her name meant purity, but that word did not truly describe her, for she was not pure of envy. Standing in her black and white waitress uniform in one of the most extravagant restaurants in the five-star hotel where she worked, she had no intention of paying attention to the tasks she was performing, for in her head, she had other roles to play.

Her daily duties were only background static to what she was really doing, for she devoted most of her brain capacity to imagination. By observing the different guests that came and went by, she lived many different lives, all of which she wished she had instead of her own. On a daily basis, she watched people that interested her with great concentration. Having done this for years, she was now the master of living vicariously through other people.

She watched most intently the married couple sitting to her left. They were not necessarily the most attractive couple, but the way they teased their two children and talked and laughed stirred a violent longing deep within her. She was expert enough not to seem obvious as she stared at them hungrily in hurried glances. In her head, though, *Safaa* was the wife most valued and adored by the loving husband who spared nothing in his expense to make her life as comfortable as possible. *Safaa* was the sole object of his attention and looks of appreciation and love, *Safaa* was the one who was scanning the menu for anything she longed to eat without dwelling on the expenses. *Safaa* was the person being lovingly embraced by the youngest child clinging to her like she was her entire world.

Only when the charming family had left did she snap out of it and realize who she really was. The realization came with less disappointment than it usually did; she had become immune to that feeling and dismissed it with ease.

Scanning around for more customers to live through, she saw the most elegant couple she had laid eyes on in maybe a month, walk into the restaurant. For the next hour, she always went around the perimeter of their table to observe them freely, and it was a successful strategy. It seemed like they were too engrossed in each other to even notice her petite waitress frame around them so very often.

Through her frequent scans, she found out they were engaged by the look of the glimmering rings on their fingers, and she could feel the large open pit in her stomach burn. She dismissed all these negative feelings and ushered her imagination to enter their lives. Suddenly *she* was the breathtakingly beautiful woman so confident and easygoing, staring into the striking hazel eyes of her fiancé. *She* was the one wearing the elegant blouse and high heels, as she sat comfortably planning the tiniest details of their wedding and life together. He had brought her flowers this morning when he picked her up to take her on this date, and all of it was a surprise. *She'd had no idea!* In her fiancé's eyes, *she* was the love of his life, and his grand romantic gestures would never cease to amaze her, and she could swear she felt his tender hands brush against her own. But in reality, they weren't. They never would.

Lost in her train of imaginary thought, she was interrupted by her fellow waitress and friend's tap on the shoulder, and with it the unmistakable sound of gum being chewed as loudly as was possible. Bassant stood next to Safaa, uttering her high-pitched screech of a laugh, which always reminded Safaa of a chicken being slaughtered.

"What are you paying so much attention to?" Bassant teased.

"You know exactly what."

"I do, actually. I came here for a better look. Is he even real? He looks like a guy from a Turkish series. If we had that girl's luck, we wouldn't be here, but then again we don't look like her."

Safaa always admired how Bassant could talk about their luckless fate with so much humor. "You're so right. We need a lot of Botox."

"You don't even need that anymore. You already got the ring! Leave the sadness to me," joked Bassant.

Safaa was about to confide in her about what she had desperately wanted to talk about since her engagement, but felt too sorry for herself to say it out loud.

Interrupting the uncomfortable moment, the manager of the restaurant materialized before them, as if out of thin air.

"I'm so sorry to interrupt you, ladies, but would you like me to bring you two glasses of cold lemonade?" he said with that famous twitch in his left eye.

"No, Mr. Magdy," said Safaa. "We were just about to leave." She could not afford to lose her job if she was about to be burdened with the expenses of furnishing a new apartment to get married. Her parents couldn't afford everything.

"And you," he said, grimacing, "throw that gum away *immediately*, do you hear me?"

And then, as if he was struck by a spell, his expression transformed into a calm, welcoming smile for the customers, and he was off. Bassant looked back at Safaa and made her usual mocking facial expression. With that, the two were forced to part ways. Safaa, thankfully, was left once more to the much more pleasant companionship of her lively imagination for the remaining working hours.

When the clock struck six, Safaa's shift was over. She walked out of the luxurious restaurant into an equally extravagant hallway and headed for the backroom. Today, however, the hallway was much more crowded than usual. Waiters and staff buzzed back and forth, carrying all sorts of items, seemingly on an urgent mission.

Curiosity overtook Safaa as she followed a flustered worker carrying more chairs than he should across the hallway. The grand ballroom was the scene of an event in the making. The staff were carefully arranging chairs, tables and centerpieces across the space. *There is going to be a wedding here tonight.*

In the past, this realization would have probably brought her immense excitement. But now, all she could do was remember the way her younger self thought of weddings and mourn her childish innocence. She never forgot the way she felt the first time she attended a wedding as a little girl.

Twenty years ago, an eight-year-old Safaa had stood at the foot of a staircase leading up to one of the many rooms dedicated to events in a much more modest venue. She felt uncontainable excitement wearing a puffy pink dress with her hair swept up with artificial flowers around a glistening bun. The shopping process had been great fun, even with her impatient mother dragging her through the stores. She was elated as she tried on the dresses and hadn't wanted to stop. In every fitting room, she would spin and spin, enjoying the fluttering movement of each dress. It reminded her of the princess movies she loved to watch so much. They all wore dresses like the ones she was trying on when they danced with their princes. Eventually, much to her equal excitement and disappointment, the preparation had come to an end, and she was about to attend a wedding for the first time.

When she walked through the venue, she felt nervous as she didn't know what to expect. Her father reached for her hand, and his grasp calmed her and made her feel more confident. A large open door invited her in, and she stepped inside. To her eight-year-old eyes, it seemed gigantic. Numerous round tables were covered in shimmering white tablecloths, each decorated with an identical large flower display in the middle and garnished with plates and utensils, as well as a few candles. Somewhere in the middle of all of it was an empty dance floor. Only a few people were sitting down on the chairs which were all decorated identically with shimmering red ribbons. The place looked mesmerizing, but something was bothering her.

"Baba, where are all the people?" she asked.

"They're coming, sweetheart. Egyptian weddings tend to start a bit late," he said.

As she was listening intently to her father's explanation, she spotted a slightly higher platform than the rest of the ballroom. It had two heavily detailed gold chairs, and behind them was a large orange, red, and white flower display intertwined with huge leaves on a wooden stand that resembled an artist's easel. The same flower decorations were on either side of the platform, only smaller.

"What is that?" she exclaimed, pointing excitedly at it.

"That is the *kosha*," replied her mother. "It's where the bride and groom will sit."

Safaa's eyes were glued to the *kosha*, as her mother had called it. She thought it was magical. The whole thing was. The bride and groom would look like a prince and princess sitting on their thrones.

Gradually, the ballroom started to fill up. People of different ages and appearances breezed past her, some of which stopped to greet her parents and upon seeing her would say things like, "Is that your daughter? *Masha' Allah,* she is so pretty. You're growing into a beautiful bride." Young Safaa basked in their attention, although she could have done without their wet kisses and lipstick stains.

When the bride and groom entered the ballroom, accompanied by loud drums, oboes, and folklore songs, she observed that all eyes were upon them, and wanted to be the beautiful woman in the flowing white gown too, one day. As the night went on, she was one of the few little girls lost in the midst of the dance floor, trying to imitate how the women were dancing. She danced and jumped in the middle of all the shimmering dresses and the bold black tuxedo pants that bombarded her on each side. As the clock hit 1 a.m., she started to become drowsy. While her father carried her down the staircase, sleep overcame her.

However, with every wedding that followed since she had grown up into a young woman, the experience could not have been more different. She felt her mother's growing anxiety as she watched other people's daughters, one after the other, get married and not her own. Her mother had started pushing her to attend more weddings in hopes of attracting an appropriate suitor there, or perhaps a future mother-in-law in search of a bride for her son. The burden of looking pretty enough to meet a possible suitor's standards became heavier and heavier on Safaa.

With every passing year, going to weddings became a chore she must do to appease her parents. Putting on makeup and dressing up had lost its appeal, and looking at the *kosha* knowing what probably went on behind the scenes to get there made it look less like a magical place and more like a bland achievement. The way people around her got there was not the love story she had always envisioned.

Now, the same Safaa stood before another ballroom, feeling nothing like the little girl in her memories did. It was as if she were remembering another lifetime with someone else and not herself at all. In the years that followed, that girl had grown up, and the reality behind the ballroom scene had become increasingly clear.

She began to discover that the pressure to reach the *kosha* was suffocating, almost as if it was all she and every girl around her were brought up to achieve.

She walked away from the ballroom and headed for the staff changing rooms at the back. She whipped out her outdated phone and began typing a text message to her fiancé.

"Can we please go out anywhere together if of course you are free? It doesn't have to be expensive or cost anything at all. We can just walk along the corniche, anything you choose."

While she changed, she heard the familiar buzzing sound and held her breath as she clicked the message open.

"We talked about this before, Safaa. You know I work hard and I am tired. I would rather spend this time resting."

When she read his reply, she immediately regretted having sent the message. How could she be so naive? Of course his answer was as it had always been and probably always would be.

She decided to reply later. For now, she only had time to dismiss the painful feeling of rejection. He was her fiancé. He was the one who was going to marry her, so that she could keep her head held high amongst her neighbors and friends finally as a married woman. But deep inside, she knew other things mattered to her as well. Although getting engaged to her fiancé had not at all been a romantic love story, Safaa had at least expected some special moments to sate her thirst to be loved, but that never happened. Her fiancé prided himself on being a practical man. Time for feelings was not on his agenda and apparently that was not going to change. *But why do I still continue to hope?*

The first time Safaa had laid eyes on her husband-to-be was nothing special. It was just as uneventful as grocery shopping or flicking through TV channels. Yet, she remembered it exactly as it had happened.

The day had begun with a rush of excitement. The household was in a state of chaos, every family member scrambling to get something done. The tasks were divided among Safaa and her father, mother, and younger sister, Nermine, who had told Safaa she was looking for any excuse to be away from her husband and children for a while. While her father went out to buy baked sweets and chocolates, the ladies stayed behind to transform their humble apartment into a gleaming spotless surface. All day long, Safaa scrubbed, scraped, and mopped. It was exhausting work, but she didn't feel disheartened or tired. She wasn't really paying attention to any of it. It was as if her hands had taken over without direction from her brain, which was busy imagining what her groom-to-be would be like. The family friend who had suggested the groom had told them the basics of what they needed to know about him. He was a respectable engineer in a small company and had an average income. That was enough information for her parents to consider him; so that had to be enough for her too.

At one point during the tiresome cleaning process, her mother approached, still gleaming with pride and sweat. "Okay, our little bride, that's enough cleaning for you. Now go to your room and get ready. I want you to shine—I want his eyes to be incapable of leaving you."

Safaa blushed. "Yes, Mama." And she was off.

In her room and concealed from all eyes, she spun around, barely able to control her excitement. In her head, a million love songs were playing, all from different singers, from different eras. Yet they were all talking about love. She had never actually related to any of them, and yet she somehow understood what they were talking about and she had always wanted to feel it. A dream that was abandoned at her pillow every morning. Her mind wandered to all the different movies and series she had watched and wondered if her love story would be just as romantic.

She had rarely seen it in real life, though. In all the families and couples around her, there was not much love there, just a sort of invisible mutual understanding that the two were in it together until the end. At least that was the way her own parents had always behaved. Safaa knew there had to be something that was more than that. Otherwise, what would all the movies that gave her goosebumps be talking about? There had to be a source. So many questions attacked her. What would he look like? What would he think of her? Would he like her? Would he actually love her? What would she look like on her wedding day? How many children would they have? How happy would their life be together?

She dug through her closet for the nicest blouse and skirt. She had tried on several outfits, occasionally asking her mother's opinion, before selecting one she was more or less fine with. After that, she headed to her dresser and scrambled through the make-up products she owned and began to apply them. She was so nervous, her hands wouldn't stop shaking, which made making herself up almost impossible. She paused and looked at herself in the mirror instead. All her flaws stared back at her.

Earlier, when she had come back from the hairdresser, her mother had told her that her hair looked too heat-damaged. Safaa ran her short, dyed black hair through her fingers and her heart sank. She knew it was a result of having to straighten it every single week for work so there was nothing she could do about it. She let go of it. Now, her dark circles mocked her, but she needed to stay up late every night, watching any movie or series just to feel something. Then she cursed the lady who had tattooed her eyebrows on for making them too dark, but she was the cheapest Safaa could find at the time, and all the other girls were doing it.

As she looked away from her eyebrows and down at her body, she grimaced. She had chosen the loosest 'nice' shirt she had, but she could still feel the belly she hated underneath, and sucked it in. Her mother had recommended this shirt for that reason, and her comment had made Safaa feel even heavier than she already did. She had been commenting on her weight more frequently lately, so Safaa had been trying not to eat at all in front of her. *Could everyone see it on my face too?* She got out her contour stick from the dresser drawer and tried to follow the makeup tutorial she had watched the day before. She drew lines across her cheeks, her temples, her nose, her chin, hoping to God they would disappear. Then on followed the rest of the makeup products she owned, one after the other concealing most features and highlighting the rest, until the dresser looked like a crime scene.

Just as she started to apply some lipstick, the doorbell rang, and she almost drew a pink line straight down across her chin. Her heart immediately started to beat uncontrollably. Her legs were steady, or were they? She sat on her bed and looked at her palms. They were sweating, so she balled her fists and took a deep breath. She had to wait for a few minutes as her parents met the groom first and then her mother came to fetch her and they went into the kitchen together. On the way there, she sneaked a glance at the meeting in the salon. Calmly seated there were her father and the father and mother of the groom, it seemed.

She almost gasped. This was it. The moment her dreams and her ideas of romance congregated, all in one meeting, in one man.

Then she saw him.

Her heart sank a little. He was wearing a gray suit and an equally gray expression. He looked nothing like the way she had imagined her husband would. He looked quite bored and unkempt. When she voiced her opinion to her mother, she instantly regretted it.

"Don't be superficial," she said. "You shouldn't choose your life partner based on these things."

This was something Safaa found strange, coming from the woman who earlier had ordered her to try to shine so he wouldn't be able to take his eyes off of her.

Her mother handed her a silver coated tray with glasses of *sharbat* on it. It was heavier than it looked, and her hands shook for a second.

"Don't drop it! You are not going to start this occasion with a catastrophe."

As she came out of the kitchen, the mother of the groom, through gritted teeth, told Safaa she looked lovely, and when she sat next to her, she proceeded to compliment the family about the house, walls, furniture, and, repeatedly, the bride. Somewhere in the midst of the fake pleasantness of the conversation, the father of the groom swooped in to ask about Safaa's family's requirements. After a long conversation between the parents negotiating those requirements, most of which Safaa had zoned out from and daydreamed through, the groom's mother interrupted with, "Let's leave them alone for a while so that they can get to know one another."

And as if struck by lightning, the two pairs of parents headed for the balcony, leaving a flustered Safaa seated on the sofa across from her soon-to-be fiancé. She felt like they were being left together like two animals at a zoo that the zookeepers want to mate. Throughout the families' small talk, she had almost forgotten he was there. *Maybe he's shy. Perhaps he's sensitive.* His personality might possibly shine through his hard shell, so she attempted to make the first move. She got up and sat on the chair next to him. As she shifted her weight in her seat, feeling the tension course uncomfortably through her veins, she detected a smile at the corner of his lips. *Maybe I misjudged him. He could be everything I wished for.* He then craned his neck to look her full in the face. He was about to say something, she knew. She thought of all the compliments or words of love at first sight that could fill that moment with perfection.

What would he say?

She held her breath in anticipation.

Then he said, "Can you cook?"

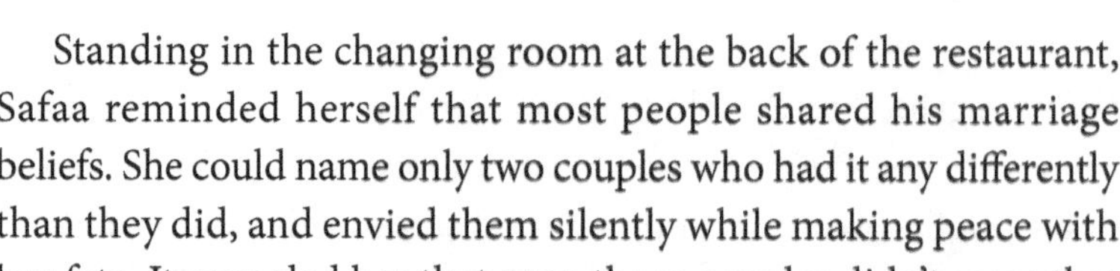

Standing in the changing room at the back of the restaurant, Safaa reminded herself that most people shared his marriage beliefs. She could name only two couples who had it any differently than they did, and envied them silently while making peace with her fate. It consoled her that even those couples didn't seem that happy either. She was not particularly beautiful, a remark made frequently by her mother, who had always advised her to cling to her fiancé and not to be foolish.

"Men do not come knocking on our door so frequently. You cannot afford to be picky. Love comes after marriage," her mother had always said.

Being the older of two daughters and the one who was not married was humiliating enough. She felt like a heavy burden on her parents and wished to relieve them as quickly as possible, so she had decided months earlier that she would do so at any expense. Even if that meant she would marry a man who didn't really feel anything towards her, much less love her.

For her dose of romance, she resorted instead to watching movies and TV shows alone at night while her parents slept. During these moments, she could get a glimpse of what it would be like to truly be loved and appreciated with romantic gestures and soft, loving words. Then at the restaurant, she got to see it all over again in real life.

At sunset, she exited the grand marble hotel, put on her headphones and pressed play on her favorite love song playlist preparing for a long way home.

Salma

In a parallel universe, her body would be painted blue only if she was so taken with the sea, that she decided to paint it across her body.

Ever so quietly, she opened the door to her children's bedroom and went inside. She held her breath, fearful of waking up her husband, who was asleep in the next room. She heard his snoring stop for a second. She paused, her heart forgetting to function. Then, he started to snore again.

Breathe out.

She closed the door behind her. There they were, huddled together in the narrow bed, keeping each other warm. Her daughter, Rokaya, had her arm over her two little brothers, forming a frail version of a protective barrier. Being the oldest sibling, Rokaya had started to notice what was happening around her. Salma could see the attempt to make sense of it all in Rokaya's wide brown eyes which had never quite changed from the day they opened for the very first time in Salma's arms. Lately, it was becoming harder and harder for Salma not to notice that her little baby daughter had made it her personal mission to watch over her younger brothers even while they were all sleeping.

Whenever they were around, Salma put on a brave face and tried to smile, but the older Rokaya got, the more she could see beyond the crumbling mask that Salma had created to protect her. At just nine years old, Rokaya was already too mature for her age and it made Salma's heart ache, painfully, for a childhood that was cut too short. That was the last thing she ever wanted. Salma remembered a day after one of the almost daily fights when Rokaya had come to her while she sat in a chair on the balcony in a state of unawareness and hugged her. That was all she had in her power to do, but the amount of love that emanated from her daughter's embrace was enough to summon tears to her eyes which Salma had quickly tried to cover up. As she stood in the bedroom now, Salma watched them with a loving gaze that was full of love and anguish, knowing they were the things she loved most in the world, and also the ones tying her to this state of despair.

It was always at this time of day that she found herself again, her real self, not what anyone wanted her to be. With the crack of dawn, her soul awakened, just for a little while, maybe because there were no voices around her except the whisper of silence and the reassurance of bird song. Every day, Salma made sure she woke up with the birds, no matter how many hours of sleep she got, just so she could exist as herself for a little while. That is, until sounds of feet shuffling began in the house, because then she had to make her own wants and needs instantly disappear.

Her dreams of being a doctor were now long behind her. They seemed so far-fetched now that she wondered how they differed from dreams of magic and of witchcraft. The light of dawn also reminded her of the long telephone calls she used to have with the man that was now her husband; telephone calls that were full of empty promises and feigned words of love. At the time, she was only a freshman college student so eager, and so naïve. The world in her eyes was messy but full of potential. She saw potential in herself as easily as she detected it in other people. And she had seen it in him. He was the first man who was brave enough to pursue her when others were too threatened by her aura of strength and confidence. She felt important and adored, and she admitted to herself that she loved to be the focus of his utmost attention. After all, out of all people, the well-known professor had chosen her. He wouldn't take no for an answer, it was not in his dictionary or his vocabulary or his behavior or probably even his DNA, and this remained the case to this day many years later. He had lured her in like the sea beckons the sun into its dark icy depths down to its death.

When she introduced Tarek to her parents as the person she chose to spend her life with, her parents welcomed him with open arms. A doctor *and* a person their daughter loved, they couldn't ask for more. Everything in Salma's memory after that was a blur. Her life had started to change faster than she could even realize. The days seemed identical yet different, compromises were forced out of her in months? Weeks? Seconds? She didn't know. Her identity was put on hold for what she thought would be a while. He had assured her of that, and she had believed him. She dropped out of medical school because he said it would get in the way of their early married life together and promised her she would finish what she started later when she got the chance. But she never did. He made sure of that. They had moved together from Cairo to Alexandria for his new job, so she was cut off from everything she ever had ever known and everyone she had ever loved. There, the truth walked out of its hiding place, then, slowly but surely, took over her life.

Salma realized that she had been frozen to her spot for too long and her legs were numb. She gently sat at the edge of her children's bed. Her head hurt. *Was it the weight of a headache or the weight of the memories?* She brought her head down to her hands. As soon as they had moved in together, it was like she never knew him, the man that she had fallen in love with didn't exist. He demanded to be fed and pampered as and when he felt like it, and even with her whole life revolving around the house and its residents and catering to their every need, he still found things to complain and fight about. No matter how hard she tried, she couldn't make it stop.

Through his eyes, her body was his own now, and he demanded it whenever he felt like it, using religion and culture to justify his right to use it, touch it, own it. She often couldn't tell how she was different from ordinary house tools, like a mop or a tele vision remote.

"It's your religious duty," he would always say, but she never understood how the body she had lived in for twenty-seven years didn't belong to her anymore whenever he felt like using it for a while.

She could recall the few occasions in her early rebellion when he used to slap her right across the face, leaving an astonished and bewildered remains of a woman in his wake, but she would forgive him when he apologized, wanting to believe, more than anything in the world, that it was a one-time thing. But it never was. *It never was.*

 In the years that followed, he had turned her body into a cruel painting of blue, purple, and red, just like a galaxy, which may have been why she kept getting lost within herself, into a world of her own.

Whenever he watched TV, he would call her in to listen to his favorite '*sheikh*' making a guest appearance on popular TV shows to give his advice. A woman called in to say that her husband was in the habit of beating her; Salma held her breath the way she used to back in school when the teacher called her name. Then she heard him address the host and the audience saying that women were by nature prone to exaggeration, and advised her to stay with her husband because "your husband feeds you and no one will marry a woman with kids."

It was a favorite pastime of her husband to make her watch this man, cackling at his sarcastic commentary, basking in his hatred and erasure of the humanity of women. He saw in him what he believed himself. At the end of these TV programs, he would tell her how grateful she should be because of how great a husband he was, after which he would sleep peacefully. Meanwhile, she didn't remember the last time she had slept through the night.

Salma would comply and keep her head down as much as she possibly could, but angering Tarek was inevitable. After a year or so, when he felt like Salma had become numb to any pain he could inflict with his hands, feet or any device in his vicinity, he started a new tactic. He threatened her with their kids. His favorite sentence had become "Don't trouble my mind if you want to keep your children by your side."

She knew that in doing so, he felt not the slightest hint of guilt. His beliefs were shared by many others, she had known it, but how could she have been so naïve as not to have noticed the signs? Every day she asked herself and every day she failed to get an answer. Every day she blamed herself and every day she hated the day she was born even more. Her body's ability to create happiness had gone, no matter how hard she tried she couldn't remember what it felt like, or imagine that she could feel it again. She wished more than anything that she would just stop existing. She knew what this was, it was the mental illness of depression, but no amount of learning and reading about it in the past had prepared her for the actual thing. It was a stronger pain than any of Tarek's beatings. His beatings were nothing compared to the emptiness that filled her insides, weighing down on her chest and slashing, as if with a knife, right at her core. It was physical and mental pain the likes of which she had never felt before. It hurt her to exist.

She had thought more than a million times of calling her parents, asking for their help, imploring them to take her back. She pictured that moment a hundred times each day. She would be at her home, her mum in one of her brightly colored home *galabeyas*, and her father in his favorite pinstriped pajamas, which he had had ever since she could remember because he didn't believe in spending any money on himself, just his family. And they would be just like they used to, emitting safety and love; and she would cry all the pain away right there in their arms until she felt safe again. But the humiliation and the guilt were too much for her to handle. The shame of being the oldest daughter, the strong daughter, who never weakened before a situation, bowing down to abuse and pain. It made her disgusted with herself. Besides, what could they do about it? She could never leave because she knew Tarek, she knew what he was capable of. She knew that he had status and connections. And if she were to speak, she might never see her children again, and no one, especially not her modest and kind mother and father, who had no notable connections to get them through life, could do anything about it.

And so, Salma put on a brave face whenever they came to visit from Cairo and pretended to be fine, but she could feel the worried gaze of her mother searching deeper into her facial expressions, and so Salma would smile faintly in her direction or make a joke, tugging at her long sleeves covering any evidence of her reality.

It took most of her willpower not to cave in and weep in her embrace, but she had so far succeeded in her self-destructive illusion. Whenever her mother would hug her grandkids, Salma would look at them, tears in her eyes, stopped by nothing but a towering dam of fear.

There was only one time when she had managed to speak the words she didn't have enough courage to say to herself, and it was to an old friend that Tarek had approved of. They sat at a restaurant, having lunch and catching up. For a brief moment, she got lost in the sweet taste of old memories and forgot the bitter one of her present.

The gentle hum of a place busy with other souls, the occasional laughs that made a brief appearance. It was a feeling she had forgotten, being with people. She could not remember the last time she had really laughed. It had probably been years. She could not relate to any of the people around her. To them, she would seem like any other middle-class woman, a confident woman, she would not seem like the 'Ramadan series version' of a domestic violence victim. That is, when they actually showed victims as victims.

"So how is Rokaya?"

"As mature as ever." She laughed. The action hurt. It didn't feel natural. Her body rejected it.

"And how's Tarek?"

Salma almost choked on her coffee, and her friend hastily handed her a bottle of water.

"Sorry."

"You're apologizing for choking?" She had a worried expression on her face.

"Tarek is fine, *al hamdulillah*." Salma's eyes welled up with tears

"Is there something you're not telling me?" When Salma looked down, Mona insisted. "What is it?"

"He ... Tarek. He hits me."

As Salma looked up, she saw that Mona visibly didn't know what to say.

"How bad is it?"

"Bad."

"I don't know what to tell you … I'm so, so sorry. I can't believe it. You seemed so happy."

"I don't remember the last time I was happy."

Mona looked confused. She paused, as she obviously did not know what to do. Then she got up and hugged Salma.

Salma saw the curious looks from people around them and suppressed the sobs threatening to spill years of pain out of her right there. But she didn't hug her friend back, so Mona sat back down eventually.

"So what are you thinking of doing?"

"Nothing. I have children. They need a father." She held her breath. *Tell me to leave. Tell me to leave please. No don't tell me to leave. I wouldn't know what I would do.*

"Salma…"

"I can't leave. You know how well-connected Tarek is. He threatens to take the kids away from me almost every single day whenever I protest."

"I can't believe this!"

Salma simply looked down, not knowing what to say.

"Salma, I know you're afraid, but you can't live like this. Your children can't live like this as well."

"Stop judging me. I am telling you, I have thought of everything. There is nothing I can do. And you can't tell a soul. Please. You don't know what he's capable of."

And so Salma survived by transforming her days into a series of tasks for the kids, her husband, and the home, and her grip on the person she used to be loosened more and more each day. Her days were mindless. Not because she wanted them to be, but because she needed them to be.

Task. Task. Task.

Sleep. Sleep. Sleep.

Task. Task. Task.

Repeat.

Rokaya shuffled in her bed. It jolted Salma physically and shoved her straight out of her thoughts.

It's fine. It's just Rokaya, just Rokaya, she thought, calming herself like a scared child.

Suddenly her stomach lurched. She felt nauseated and even though she was going to throw up, she tiptoed to the bathroom. Closing the door behind her, she hugged the toilet for the next five minutes. In the midst of throwing up, she noticed something. Her period pads were next to the sink. *Tarek hates it when they are visible.*

Then it hit her so fast that she imagined this is what a car accident would feel like.

Two lines on a pregnancy test confirmed her deepest fear.

As the lines appeared into the realm of reality, something deep inside Salma took over her.

One more soul born into this pain.

One more piece of him.

One more thing to keep me here.

Putting on her prayer *esdal* and coat over her nightgown, she ever so softly unlocked the apartment door and descended the stairs. Her body had acted without her orders and she found herself going straight to where she could always feel beauty around her whenever she felt as if it were no longer possible.

After a half-hour walk, she was there, with two slippers in one hand and two cold feet on the sand walking across the sandy beach. The Alexandrian sea welcomed her with a loud crash on an expectant shore, producing a shower of glittering white foam, before retreating right back to where it came from.

The still-deserted beach was the only place she had felt truly at home in a strange city, and she sat at the edge trying to summon that feeling now. If anyone could see her at that moment, they would stare in confusion at the peculiar situation, a barefoot woman in a coat and prayer *esdal* standing on the beach at dawn like a ghost. The breeze was painfully cold against her cheeks, but she relished the feeling, it meant that she was still alive. She wondered how many other faces that same wind had touched before her own, and more importantly, how many happy moments were graced with its presence. *What did happiness feel like?*

She remembered her first ever trip to the beach, it was one of those hazy memories. She could vaguely recall a few words spoken to her and a lot of the feelings that overwhelmed her, and yet, it was one of her fondest memories. Her older cousins were there, acting as role models for her first time beach experience. As the adults lingered back setting up the seating area under the umbrella, the kids ran forward, fearless. At the edge of the waves, her oldest cousin turned to her.

"People will tell you to swim deeper into the sea where it's calmer and easier to flow through, but know this, all the fun is right here at the edge, if you can conquer the Mediterranean's waves, you can conquer anything," he had said with a mischievous grin, which was startlingly white against his sun-tanned summer skin.

The waves came in one after the other, meeting the shore with a loud threatening crash. In a hidden corner of her mind she was a little afraid, but mostly she felt energized and alive. Then one after the other the five cousins went in, it was hilarious to watch because the waves were the strongest at the very beginning and they fell quite a few times in an attempt to enter further. When it was finally her turn, and her feet met the salt water, right then, she didn't have a care in the world. They spent the next few hours waiting for each wave to approach them, and then they would jump as high as they could and conquer the wave. They were young and they had nothing to fear. They still had a large craving for life and so in these early battles, they dived freely and without wounds. The world in her eyes seemed so huge and yet she didn't think it was scary at all. Her imagination told her all she needed to know, and she floated on the comfort that the world was a good kind of limitless.

That was Salma's last memory of being completely fearless. As the years went by, life taught her fear. The scary things were never the deep seas or the crashing waves or even the monsters she used to imagine when the shadows walked across her bedroom walls at night, but the monsters that might be lurking inside other people.

Was Tarek a monster? Had she known deep down that he was a monster? In the number of hours she had spent asking herself these questions over the years, she could have gotten her degree.

But he apologizes when I cry. He kisses my forehead when I make him dinner. He says he loves me. He buys me flowers on Mother's

Day. He says he will work on controlling his anger if I stop provoking him. He always promises he won't hit me again.

But he hits me again.

He always hits me again.

She didn't understand how she let it happen. Again and again and again. The truth was, she despised who she was now. As much as she blamed her husband for her cruel life, she blamed herself more for letting it happen. A lot of people would blame her and ask her why she hadn't left. But he had this effect on her, his very presence belittled her, made her feel worthless, microscopic, invisible, absent, and she evaporated into the wind.

He had made it his life's purpose to kill every last droplet of confidence or dignity she hid deep within her, until all that was left was this empty shell drifting through the house like a barely noticeable cloud of dust. On her very limited trips outside her house, mostly to buy groceries she wondered if people's eyes could see right through her skin and straight to her very core and know how pathetic she really was, her veins and arteries caked with cowardice, it made her sick. *She made herself sick.*

For a brief moment, she pictured it happening. She would walk straight to the waves that flirtatiously whispered to her in menacingly hushed tones. Let its cold liquid grip numb each body part as she walked forward. She would forget it all, let the feeling of complete surrender take charge, all the way to the tip of her head, and then let go of herself, of her memories, of the pain.

Maybe the salt water would wash the blue on her skin away.

She closed her eyes and tried to summon the courage to do it.

But one thing tied her feet to the ground; she could almost hear their innocent laughter pierce her heart, and she couldn't let go because they needed her, and she needed them even more. She had brought them into this world, and she would protect them with her life until the day she left it.

As the sun began to rise higher into the sky, she became surer and surer of herself and of her decision.

She would sneak away, take her children, leave a brief note to her husband telling him to let them go, even though she knew for sure this would not be the end of it, and go back to Cairo. She would either pay a brief visit to her family, or start a new life altogether. Hide somewhere he wouldn't find her. She searched within herself for anything that emotionally linked her to that place. She cleared her head and tried and tried again, but no, that place didn't feel like home and that man was everything she had come to hate.

She headed back down the abandoned street to her prison silently praying to God that he was still asleep.

Mariam
Part Three

My time in the apartment, where I first woke up in this bodiless state, seems like an eternity ago, and so does the beginning of my endless wandering in Cairo. But how much time has actually passed, I have no idea. One of the blessings of being in this form, whatever it is, is that I have no concept of time. Even if I did, why would it matter to a dead person? Time is a subject of worry only to the living, and I am grateful that this is now behind me.

Even though I long to stay oblivious, more comes back to me.

I feel more like myself than I have in a very long time. I recognize traits in myself that I thought had long disappeared creeping into me again, as if all this time they had simply been hiding underneath the bed or behind the curtains. I long to watch people, to talk to them, to learn their stories. I want to know why they are the way they are. If their parents had been kind and if their houses feel like home. If they feel more like a bird or a butterfly. I have become curious, just like the five-year-old version of me, and the more I immerse myself in other people's lives, the more life is breathed back into mine, and I remember more. I remember the burst of energy of the child I had been, always running around at an alarming speed, jumping everywhere, pestering people with questions even if they were strangers. I remember how the light within me dimmed and faltered as the years went by. I remember that there was a time when it went out completely for the last time, but I can't, or perhaps I refuse to, remember why. But like everything in life, it was not up to me. I can't stop my thoughts from reeling.

I need a distraction.

And what better distraction from my problems is there than those of others.

The metro is more crowded than I remember it to be. Maybe it is one of those inexplicably busy hours when Egyptians decide to leave the shade of their homes and roam the earth. My surroundings are a haze of faces, watching, waiting.

I look at the sea of eyes before me, with a few variations in color and even less in expression. All watching, waiting. For what, I do not know. I want to yell at them to start living, but I know people do not realize what they waste until the days and the seconds are numbered. It is the way they were made. Perhaps only the lucky ones can break free from the numbing trance of routine.

I head to the women-only passenger car because I know countless souls would be packed in there, like pickled tuna, just to avoid being in close proximity to a potentially handsy male stranger.

Turns out, I am right.

So many women are sitting and standing, awaiting their destination. They are all wearing that same look of waiting, whether they are sitting still, talking on the phone or chatting animatedly to someone else. And this act of waiting somehow unifies them, bridging the gap created by the differences in their appearance.

I look around, scanning the sea of faces, hungry for distraction. The first thing that immediately catches my attention is a girl wearing a traditional farmer's *galabeya*, which is an unusual sight in Cairo. But that isn't even the most interesting thing about her. Even from a distance, I can see she has dazzling blue eyes, a shade of which I have never seen before. The color reminds me of the clearest and happiest of blue skies. When I come closer to the girl, however, my perspective changes. Because even though she looks really young, her eyes hold so much pain. They are wide with fear and swimming with tears. She looks like she is trying to hold the tears back, but finally they drip onto her lap, one after the other.

Right now, I wish I had a body, for I would have headed straight to that girl and told her, with no introductions, that everything, everything is going to be alright. But right now, I am nothing, and even though she is right there, more than distance separates us. I anxiously scan her surroundings, hoping that someone else sees her and helps her.

Then, I notice a woman sitting on the opposite seat, looking at the girl through her bright blue glasses and voluminous wild brown curly hair. The woman seems to hesitate, as if contemplating whether or not to get up, and I hope with everything in me that she approaches the little girl.

She does.

The woman with the blue glasses gets up and crouches down in front of the girl in the *galabeya* so that they are face to face. She puts the girl's hands in her hands and asks her what's wrong. If I could cry tears of joy, I would. I don't know if I had been brave enough in my past to do what this woman was doing right now.

I look away, knowing that this woman has the ability to handle the situation.

A quick glance stops me at where a lot of the women are staring. At a young woman who seems like the human embodiment of a storm. What demands my attention immediately is the self-assertive way in which she carries herself and her shock of medium-length burgundy-red hair standing out in the sea of women in the metro. How she manages to walk in the streets looking so unique and obvious without fear of harassment, I do not know. A number of women stare at her disapprovingly and mockingly, and I can hear two of them exchanging loud comments about her nose ring, as if profanity itself was clinging to her face. They seem as though they want to be heard by her. But if she did in fact hear them, the young woman doesn't show it. She continues to look determinedly ahead, as if they meant nothing to her. I see in this woman a person I could have been, or wish I had been, but knew I never was.

I am thankful then when the brightness of a nearby screen catches my attention and distracts me from thoughts of my past self. The owner of the phone is another young woman. She is wearing a white *hijab* and a blazer to match and she has a straight posture that screams confidence. She is grasping onto the metro pole with one hand, and holding a phone with the other. The whole look of her emits the glow of a healthy soul. She seems entirely fine, until her phone rings. When she sees who the caller is, she rolls her eyes. I watch curiously as the glow around her darkens significantly after that. I wonder whose name on that bluish bright screen causes her so much pain.

Eventually, I look away from the woman in the blazer and direct my attention to a woman with a pixie haircut. At some point, I wish I were bold enough to cut my own lengthy hair off, but could never bring myself to do it. My hair has been something to hide behind all my life. The woman is wearing a loose white blouse and patterned pants. Everything about her is colorful and interesting. She even has a few splatters of paint on the back of her hand. I could have watched this woman for hours. She sits there, studying people on the metro as if taking their specific measurements, and I long to strike up a conversation with her and become her friend. But that is an experience I would never get to have again.

A swish of a ponytail demands my attention next. A pretty, young woman dressed casually in a white t-shirt is sitting with her hands balled into fists. She has a tangible air of defeat about her. She closes her eyes and shakes her head left to right as if dismissing a thought or memory. Her phone dings, probably signaling the arrival of a text message. She seems to exhale in relief when reading its contents. But, curiously enough, her soul still remains troubled. I long to know more. I watch her for a while. Suddenly, she gets up and offers her seat to a girl in a school uniform. I wonder why she chooses to do so when she doesn't seem fine herself, until I see the girl's face.

There is nothing in particular that is noticeable about the girl except for how unnoticeable she seems to want to be. Everything about her body language is weak, from her head hanging low or her arms folded around her torso. The light around her is very dim and faltering, bright for a second, almost gone the next. I know her soul is in danger. She declines the woman's offer, almost in fear, and seems adamant on looking away and into space, at nothing in particular. Somehow, I know she is trying to escape in her mind. I know because at one point I had been her, just like her, young, much too young, and hopeless. This memory hurts me, not in the physical sense but a different kind of pain, and I redirect my gaze defiantly.

Loud joyous laughter demands my attention next. A woman in a dirt-covered *abaya* and torn shoes is hugging a giggling little girl who could be no older than twelve wearing a fading green t-shirt and pajama pants. From the way they are dressed, they seem like they might be living or working on the street, and the mood that envelopes them is contagiously positive. After the hug, the girl speaks excitedly to the older woman, whom I assume to be her mother. But from where she was stationed, I couldn't hear what was being said. The little girl's blissful smile emits warmth and strength that seems to touch me, and the halo around her is thankfully as bright as a child's should be. The little girl clings to a doll in a way that brings joy to my heart. It brings me a sense of comfort I haven't felt in a long time.

The metro jolts as if the wheels have come across a momentary obstacle. A petite woman almost crashes into the place where my body would have been. The woman quickly apologizes to no one in particular and grabs a neighboring pole. She then replaces the headphones, which had fallen out, back into her ears. Her short jet-black hair covers her face, but when she brushes it off, her eyes lock on one of the women and stay there for a long time. I spend a few moments trying to make out her feelings, but can't. I eventually look away, hungry for more lives to distract myself with.

Opposite to where that woman is standing is an adorable little boy, sound asleep on a girl's shoulder, blissfully unaware it seems. She, on the other hand, is quite awake, wrapped in a sort of confusion. She seems like a little girl who was just starting to wake up to the reality of something. With her arm around both children and a toddler on her lap is a woman who seems to be their mother. Nothing about her is particularly special or distinguishable at first glance. Her existence is like a shadow or a cloud of dust that could, just as easily as dandelion seeds, be blown away by a gentle breeze. Looking more closely, however, brings me to a halt. The bruises on her arm and the defeated way in which she holds herself are nothing compared to her eyes.

Because they are completely and utterly empty.

Her eyes are a void that compels you to look into the nothingness within. There is no strength, no hope, no life left in those eyes. They merely show you her defeated soul which did not so much as give off a fickle glow.

It had been extinguished.

No matter how hard I try, I can't look away. I can't tear my attention from her eyes because, I realize, they look exactly like mine, down to the last gritty hopeless detail. These were exactly my eyes for a long time. Before I … took my own life.

Surrounded by so many souls I drown into the depths of my own and begin to remember.

I was living the memory, I was choking on it, and it forced my head under water.

Mariam
Part Four

I remember it in fragments. Glimpses of events, and a flood of feelings. For days, maybe weeks after it had happened, memories kept coming back to me. As if my body was just registering it for the first time.

I was fifteen.

Up until that day, I would have called myself a sheltered child. A happy child. Yes, a child. Because I looked at the world with the same wonder a child would. Of course, I knew there were bad things in the world. That women suffered. That the world could be cruel, I would have been blind not to notice. But not this cruel.

I remember it was a Friday, because we always visited family on Fridays. But that day, I didn't feel well. So I stayed home. Sometimes I wonder how different my life would have been if I hadn't. But that was like imagining being a completely different person, in a parallel universe.

I heard the doorbell, and I crept up to the door because my parents taught me not to let anyone know if I was home alone. But it wasn't a stranger. It was my cousin. My cousin who had known me since I was a baby. He was the oldest of my cousins, twenty-five at the time, and his father, my father's oldest brother. I recall feeling confused because my parents were supposed to be at their house right now.

I opened the door to greet him.

The last thing I clearly remember about it was him at that door. There was probably small talk after that, but it doesn't exist in my memory, or my brain has erased it. I just remember the bruises and the blood and glimpses of the aftermath. I see them in bursts. Like a movie scene.

"Don't tell anyone or I'll tell it my way."

These were his words to me after it happened. These were also the words that echoed inside me ceaselessly, breaking every part of me as they persevered and persevered, just as loud, never weakening in power, causing my destruction. Nothing seemed to stop them. They traveled from my ears down to my spine and into my heart, and it stopped being anything but a beating organ torturously keeping me alive.

Everything had been a blur, but everything after that was even less clear. I remember having to tell my parents when they got home because they found me unconscious and bleeding on the floor. I didn't even have a chance to hide it like he had wanted me too. My body couldn't handle it. It broke down. He had probably panicked and left me there. Hoping that he had scared me enough into silence. Or maybe the shame of it would. *Blank.* Going home from the hospital, sitting in my bed, and staring into space. *Blank.* My mom saying something that seemed miles away. Like a distant floating message meant for someone other than me. *Blank.* My dad arguing with my mom when she wanted to report it to the police. *Blank.* My dad coming into my room one day. Telling me never to speak of this to anyone. *Blank.* My mom entering my room one day. Her trying to get me to talk but crying instead. *Blank.* My dad shaking his head like a child's toy that had been broken. *Blank.* He looked at me like I had changed somehow. Like I wasn't the same daughter anymore. *Blank.* My dad avoiding eye contact with me. *Blank.* I forgot what his eyes look like. *Blank.* His asking me what I had expected when I opened the door to a man when I had been home alone. *Blank.*

I only barely heard any of it, but even if I could speak I doubted he would understand it when I told him I expected to be treated like a human being, because even I struggled to believe my logic now. All of these memories seemed like they belonged to someone else.

And somehow, they did.

Because that day had changed me. I was no longer the girl who believed that life was an adventure and that people were good. That was a dead girl now.

They tried to get me to go to school, but I couldn't breathe standing between my mother's arms at the gate because I felt like he was somewhere in this world with his friends, laughing together, moving on with his life, and I had died a thousand deaths because of him. I couldn't get myself to move. There were people my age there, with concerns that seemed trivial to me now and young dreams that I found laughable. I felt I was miles away, staring at them, a translucent barrier between us. I was tainted and they were not. I was broken and they were not. I was shameful and they were not.

I heard my parents arguing about letting me see a therapist because I had stopped responding to anyone. I heard my mom pleading, but my father yelled at her that no daughter of his was going to a place for crazy people and that no one can know about this. "He is my brother's son!" In those days, I heard so many things that created invisible scars scrawled across my exhausted skin. And late at night, while I would try to sleep, looking for relief, to my eyes only, those words would glow. They would glow so very brightly.

I think the reality of the situation never sank in for my father. He was like a man cornered, trying to protect something only he could see. From a danger only he could feel. In a culture that ran in his DNA. His daughter. His only daughter. She was tainted now. The worst possible thing that could happen to a girl.

I barely registered any of this. I was busy hating him, myself, and the world.

Almost a year later, I woke up, took some pills, and waited for the pain to die with me. It was uneventful and sudden. If you had asked me a year before if this is how I pictured my life would end, I would have called you insane. And, yet there I was, pills on the nightstand, fading.

The metro whooshes forward and jolts. My surroundings haven't changed. There is the defeated woman and her two children with that fading light in her eyes. Still there. All the women are there, just as they have been.

The truth is, I could have been any of them, any of the bodies full of stories surrounding me in every direction, being written as we speak. I relate to the looks in their eyes. I can see into their souls. Sense their troubles. Feel the burden they are under. The pain.

I look around, at the women who remain seated, waiting for their own destinations under the fluorescent metro lights. I feel connected to each and every one of them, if not in appearance, then in emotions. If not in emotions, then in struggle.

Yes, we are united in struggle.

From the moment we are born, expectations are born with us. Piling up more and more as the years go by. Repeat after me, they would say. Learn your name, they would say. Learn your place, they would say. You are weak. You are here to serve. You are here to satisfy. You are less. It doesn't matter whether you live in a castle or on the roof of a crumbling building in a slum, the mantra is the same. Instilled within us through the centuries.

But no, even though I feel like we are the same. I no longer want to hide nor pretend I am anyone else. I know I am Mariam, who took her own life at fifteen.

And now, I am Mariam who wishes after re-experiencing life for the second time to have this body back enclosing me. If not to save myself, to save anyone else from it all. No one should have to feel the way I felt. No one.

I have allowed him to break me, in more ways than one, but I had simply needed support, anyone who would hold my hand

and get me to stand up straight once more and look into the eyes of people without shame. Someone to tell me it hadn't been my fault. None of it was. To fight for me.

And yet, there was no such person for me, and sadly I was unable to be that person for myself.

I wish I could be that person for someone else.

I didn't deserve what happened to me. No one around me deserves to carry the burden they so clearly do.

I have the overwhelming need to shout, to scream, so that every woman around me can hear. So that every woman on this earth could hear.

"You are more than they tell you you are. You are more. You are more. You are more."

How does no one around me feel my presence? I'm vibrating with energy. I'm glowing. I'm transforming. I am everything. I wish I were more than a dead girl right now. I wish. I hope. I crave. I desire. I feel.

Behind a woman holding onto one of the metro poles, I see a strand of curly black hair and a glimpse of a face that brings everything inside me to a halt. Some mysterious pull from within makes me maneuver around and through all the waiting women in the metro.

She reminds me of my mother.

I chase her as fast as I can, but she keeps getting farther.

Then I hear her voice. Echoing. From a mysterious place.

"Yes, the divorce is final, thank God. He wouldn't give it to me easily, but I was persistent. There was nothing left there to fight for. He just wanted to keep me because he was attached to whatever was left of our image as a family. You know, he refused to believe what happened, in the end, to Mariam."

"Thank God it's over. I never thought you'd get here. And the apartment?"

"I didn't fight for it. Too many memories I don't want to hold onto."

"I'm so sorry, Ghalya dear. I didn't mean to upset you."

"You didn't. I need to be stronger for her. I need to be able to talk about this."

"You *are* strong, my dear. You went to court. You fought her case for weeks until you won! You won for her."

"I just wish I had been stronger from the beginning. I wish I was stronger when she needed me the most."

I try to feel in every part of my being that I am fine and I forgive her.

"But I know my little girl. Her heart was so big, and she would forgive me."

Of course I would forgive you. I wish I could hold you. I wish I could cry with you.

I hear monotonous beeps.

Where is that noise coming from? I will my eyelids to open. I see more fluorescent lights, but this time coming from a spotlessly clean white ceiling. I see my mom's black curly hair. She's blurry but undeniably there above me. Her hands are clasped over her mouth and eyes crinkled at the corners, just the way I love them to be. Her childhood friend Amal, whom I had only seen in my mother's old pictures, is behind her, holding onto her arm. My mom says my name breathlessly, more a whisper than a word, and calls for the nurses.

"She heard you! She heard you!" cried Amal.

Did I live? Because if I did, I am ready for war.

In a parallel universe,
She would be free.

Acknowledgments

This book would not have been possible without the support of some extraordinary individuals. First and foremost, I am deeply grateful to my parents, who instilled in me from a young age the belief that my voice matters, and who have always supported me and my dreams. You mean everything to me. Likewise, I am grateful to my dearest grandmother, who first made me fall in love with the magic of storytelling. And to all the friends who cheered me on, you know who you are, thank you. I must also thank the exceptional Sherine Elbanhawy, who believed in this book, and in me, from day one. Furthermore, I am grateful to Amr Shehata, my editor, who helped me mold and transform this book until it reached its full potential. I could not have done this without you. And to Rana Mwafy, my book cover designer, thank you for bringing my imagination to life. Last but definitely not least, to my editor Camellia Hamdy, thank you for understanding and supporting my vision.

And to you now reading this, you have no idea how much I appreciate you.

Thank you for being here.

About the Author

Headshot by Dina Soliman

Samar Saadallah is an author and women's rights activist who currently resides in Cairo, Egypt. To keep up with her updates on social media @samarssaadallah